Grant called, and at first it wasn't that much fun. He told me how he likes his roommate, Matt, and how he's sending me pictures of his dorm room and how he got a job at a pet store this afternoon, only it's one of those giant corporate chains—not what he wanted. He went on and on. He sounded so good, so happy . . . I almost really hated him for a minute. How dare he?

Told him I couldn't do this, that I missed him too much and was coming home immediately. That I hated everything here and felt completely out of place.

"Hello? Is this Courtney Von Dragen Smith?" he said, tapping the phone. "Operator? I thought I was talking to Courtney V.D. Smith."

"Will you quit saying that?" I started laughing even though I was still crying. Nobody was allowed to use my middle initials except Grant. "Why are you saying that?"

"Because this isn't you. This really doesn't sound like you."

"The crying part? Or the whining, complaining part?"

"The giving up part. You don't give up that easily. On like, anything."

"I don't?" I asked. Shoot. Because this throwing-in-the-college-towel thing was something I felt I could be a real natural at.

ALSO BY CATHERINE CLARK:

Truth or Dairy

CATHERINE CLARK

Wurst
Case
Scenario

Harper
tempest

HarperTempest
An Imprint of HarperCollinsPublishers

Wurst Case Scenario
Copyright © 2001 by Catherine Clark
Printed in the United States of America. For information address
HarperCollins Children's Books, a division of HarperCollins
Publishers, 1350 Avenue of the Americas, New York, NY 10019.

Library of Congress Cataloging-in-Publication Data
Clark, Catherine, 1962–
  Wurst case scenario / Catherine Clark.
    p.   cm.
  Summary: Courtney, a vegetarian animal-rights activist, records in
her diary the events of the beginning of her freshman year at a
Wisconsin college, far away from Colorado and her boyfriend Grant,
surrounded by cheese- and meat-lovers.
  ISBN 0-06-029525-2 (lib. bdg.) — ISBN 0-06-447287-6 (pbk.)
    [1. Universities and colleges—Fiction.   2. Wisconsin—Fiction.
3. Vegetarianism—Fiction. 4. Diaries—Fiction.] I. Title: Wurst case
scenario. II. Title.
PZ7.C5413 Wu 2001   2001016842
[Fic]—dc21   CIP
                                                              AC

❖
First HarperTempest edition, 2001
Visit us on the World Wide Web!
www.harperteen.com

Thank you to my editor, Abby McAden, for her incredible patience, sense of humor, and insight. Many thanks to Kristin Pederson for her creative input, and to Sherren Clark for the weeks in Madison at the East Johnson Street Writing Workshop. And thanks also to Jen Gentle, Bill Gentle, Keith Wood, Anne Kerwin, Wendy Scherer, Pam Delgaty, and last, but not least, Theo.

Can I even explain the weirdness that is my life right now?

My new college roommate, the person I have to spend the next 9 months living with, Mary Jo Johannsen, is sleeping now. Went to bed at 10. Set alarm for 5 but said she'd probably wake up before it went off. What? Who wakes up before 5?

Her straw-blond hair is spread out on the pillow. She has baby-blue flannel pajamas with little black-and-white Holstein cows on them. Which she is wearing even though it is about 90 degrees in our room. 3rd floor. Hot, humid. No A/C.

Mary Jo is the type of person you might hate if she weren't so nice. Too nice, actually. Highly suspect. Has perfect body, perfect hair, and no clue of this. Wears unflattering clothes that end up looking good anyway— orange corduroy pants, the kind you see for $1.99 at Old Navy, only hers are legitimately vintage, plus white T-shirt with green John Deere tractor logo. She's tan, she has muscles. She looks healthy, strong, *normal*. Sort of like Drew Barrymore.

Me, I feel like the heifer in the photo at the end of her bed. Could be the fact I ate cheese in addition to sour cream today, however. In spite of being a vegan. Okay, a semi-vegan. Mary Jo's mom brought snacks and sand-wiches and cubed cheese and kept insisting I have some, wouldn't take no for an answer. Realized I had to take something or she would never stop asking. Opted for the lesser of 27 evils and had cheddar cubes. Mom was in heaven, bonding with other mom over advantages of having large cooler stocked with bite-size items in Ziploc.

Anyway, now my stomach is as bloated as my college application was, which is the reason I ended up with mega-size scholarship and grants to this supposedly "top-notch" Cornwall Falls College in the first place. It is *way* out in the country. Thought I would like that for some reason. Now it seems crazy as I am too far from major airports. Where is my escape route?

Never should have listened to Mom. Or guidance counselor. Or Gerry, the ex-guidance counselor. They all told me to volunteer, like being the student council VP and then P wasn't enough. End result: I cleaned out streams. I collected donated books. I tutored at elementary school. I nearly joined the Girl Scouts to get into a good college. Insane concept, as I am too old to wear uniforms and badges, not that I had any badges yet, which would have been really embarrassing. Would have been oldest living Brownie, and though I have a few camping skills, like rolling up my sleeping bag, and gathering firewood, I am lousy at camp songs and cannot cook a marshmallow without singeing my hair.

What was I thinking when I decided to go away to college? What was I thinking when I said, "Hey, okay, Wisconsin!" I even went for a tour, which should have given me time to think. But no. Must have been in a dairy-induced daze. Just because they served free

Starbucks Frappuccinos on the plane and got my vegan/vegetarian/non-chicken meal right, I took that as a sign. A flight attendant with frosted blond hair and an attitude about me having a special request meal gives me a stupid egg-free, gluten-free cookie . . . and I make a major life decision based on that? Am I *that* insane?

Anyway, that's beside the point. It's all beside the point. The point is that I am here at Cornwall Falls College.

Getting here was *so weird*. Little sign outside; Rankin Hall. Crowded parking lot. We walked up the stairs and I was wondering if Mary Jo would be here yet. Nervous about meeting her. Have never had a roommate except for Alison, and sisters don't count. Wondered if I'd filled out my housing questionnaire right, if there was such a thing as a right answer to "Hobbies You Enjoy."

What about "Hobbies You *Don't* Enjoy"? Why don't they ever ask the important questions?

Anyway, we wandered down the hall looking for 326. Very crowded. Lots of parents, lots of microwaves and computer boxes and trunks, lots of girls looking either ecstatic or terrified. I kept saying "Hi," like an automaton. Hi, hi, hi. Then suddenly we were at room 326.

I peeked around the corner. Mary Jo was standing on her bed, putting up a Faith Hill poster. Which would add to the 10 million other things she already had on the wall: barn print, family portrait, Leann Rimes calendar, and 3 different "Precious Moments" posters with uplifting sayings and supposedly cute photos of kittens and puppies.

Agh!

Mrs. Johannsen was scrubbing built-in dresser and closet with toxic cleaning product. No oxygen in room.

Mr. Johannsen was creating new furniture, putting up shelves, hammering nails into concrete, with plaster pieces crumbling to the floor which was covered with giant red University of Wisconsin rug.

"Um. Hi?" I said.

Everyone totally dropped what they were doing and turned around. Mary Jo smiled as Mom and her parents shook hands and exchanged fascinating news of trip, highway route, weather. Mary Jo said she hoped I didn't mind if she kind of got the place settled—she left all this wall space for me, and if I wanted to change beds or anything, that was completely fine, etc. Very sweet and polite. I was looking around this tiny room trying to imagine how I could make it look remotely like a place I lived when suddenly this crowd of tall blond boys came rushing at me. Thought it was some fraternity reference when Mary Jo mentioned "brothers." Then I remembered there are no frats here, and realized these were her actual brothers. 6 of them, all over age 20. Was introduced but forgot each name instantaneously as they all wore similar T-shirts and jeans and boots. They all work on the family dairy farm. They all have the blondest hair I've ever seen. They all insisted on bringing up my stuff (which was very, very cool). Only took them 5 minutes.

Mrs. Johannsen then served a huge lunch. Their giant cooler was used as a table. 6 boys perched on Mary Jo's bed; me, Mom sat on my bed across from them; Mary Jo, Mr. and Mrs. J insisted on sitting on empty cardboard boxes, which they were practically falling into. Very bizarre meal. Kept having to say I wasn't that hungry as everyone else devoured ham and cheese on white, cold fried chicken, macaroni salad, some sort of Jell-O salad made with cottage cheese and marshmallows. Bluck.

Realized boys were staring at my "Meat is Murder" anti-animal-abuse poster and my framed "Vegetarians Make Better Lovers" bumper sticker (a joke gift! It's a joke, guys!), and old "Truth or Dairy" sign from the original store (Gerry's going-away gift). Very embarrassing. But is it my fault they were gnawing on drumsticks at the time?

"Colorado! *Wow*. That's *so* far away! So how did you end up here?" Mary Jo asked. 6 brothers stared at me, awaiting answer.

I launched into the story of how Grandma and Grandpa went here, and how I was interested in environmental law, and how Cornwall Falls kept calling and adding more stuff to my financial package just to get me to accept, so it seemed like they really wanted me to come, and I told Mary Jo how at the same time I was waitlisted at Colorado College, and how it seemed like I should go somewhere where they wanted me. Etc. Too depressing to remember faulty chain of events right now.

At the same time, I was thinking about how Grandma told me I'd be a better person for accepting the challenge of moving away from home, and how Grant and I would be a better couple for it, etc., etc., blah blah blah. She snowed me. I can see that now. Don't want to see Grandma tomorrow when she and Grandpa are supposed to visit. Hate her for giving me that speech.

I'm beginning to feel very, very sorry for myself. I miss Grant so intensely right now.

Okay, so I'm going to take a deep breath and think calming thoughts. Repeat after me, Courtney: Grant and I will stay together, we are going to make this long-distance relationship work. I'm picturing happy places. Sun, mountains, gurgling streams.

What a bunch of crap. This isn't working at all.

Anyway, Mary Jo and her family were really into what I said about deciding to go to CFC. Her mother started talking about how Cornwall Falls launches this major recruitment drive to bring in students from all over the country, and how they're committed to a diverse population, which is great considering it's a small college in a rural area.

"It's known for being a microcosm of society," Mary Jo said.

"Yeah, that sounds familiar," I said. It was straight out of their shiny, misleading brochure with photos of corn-stalks. So far all I've seen are tall blond people. Microcosm of Norway, *maybe*.

Mary Jo is from a small town about two hours from here. She's going to study science and math, and she likes country-western music. I'm living with a brainy Faith Hill. Who goes to bed way earlier than me and snores, I just found out a minute ago.

It's so strange, because they did make us fill out those really long questionnaires. There are like 2,000 other students here, and Mary Jo and I are supposed to be the most compatible out of all the other people I could have been matched with? Based on what? The fact we're both 18?

I am looking around our room. It is as polarized as a plug-in. Her side: country. My side: rock 'n' roll. Her side: cows. My side: leave cows alone.

She has a serious number of knickknacks on all open surfaces. We're talking a clock shaped like a potato, and tiny porcelain lambs, and other crap like that. She put about 18 different editions of *Chicken Soup for the Soul* on her new dad-installed bookshelves (he built me some, too, which is very cool). What is the deal with those books? Souls don't need *soup*. And chicken? Definitely not. My soul wants miso soup, if anything.

Also, my soul wants to get out of here and move back home. To be with Grant. But I guess it's too soon to bail. When *would* be a good time? Must check Leann Rimes calendar.

Grandma and Grandpa came today, stopping by on their way home from 2-week tour of the Great Lakes. They were on some senior excursion where they drive around hauling trailers and all hook up at the same spot. Hook up their trailers that is. Though with my grandparents you never know. Ever since Viagra was invented, their lifestyle's gotten a lot more, shall we say, active. The less I know about it, the better.

Grandpa insisted on coming to town because he loved going to school here and wanted to show me the sights and give me the tour of town. Which took all of 10 minutes. I must have been in *such* a daze when we drove into town for our campus tour last March that I didn't really notice. Perhaps I was too out of it due to multiple Frappuccinos. Perhaps they distracted me at crucial town-viewing moments by asking me all about myself. They kept doing that. Very tricky.

First of all, when you get down to Main Street from campus (which is only about a 5-minute walk), there's a sign that says, "You're in the One and Only Wonderful Wauzataukie!" Like I wasn't painfully aware of that.

The place is like a shrine to Dairiness.

I mean it. There's a bronze statue of a guy called His Royal Dairiness in the center of town, in the park. (Cute park. Very green. Little healthy-looking kids running around, high on calcium.) The founder of the town was a dairy god, I guess. He invented the udder or something.

I also learned that the town's name is ancient—it comes from a Native American tribe's language and means "land of standing water," or something like that. Nice connection, but not exactly inspiring—sort of mildewy-sounding. Grandpa kept joking that the town is the nation's largest breeding ground for the state bird: the mosquito. Then Grandma said no, that was Minnesota's state bird. Ha ha ha. Funny. Except that right now I have too many red welts on my legs to count.

There also was a cow sculpture representing different breeds, with some bronzed goats running around the base. I don't know why cow sculptures are necessary, when cows are never out of sight and certainly never out of smell here.

Grandpa and Grandma kept lamenting the stores that have closed since they went here 100 years ago. The missing "five and dime," the vanished Bert's Dairy Bar. (Since when do you order milk at a bar? No wonder the concept failed.)

"At least good old Brat Wurstenburger's still around. If you ever want the perfect brat, that's the place to go," Grandpa said. "You can get it boiled or grilled, made with cheese or beer, you can get weisswurst and knockwurst. . . ." And he was off on another lecture about the wonders and virtues of sausage casing.

Naturally we ended up at Brat Wurstenburger for lunch. It's incredibly popular—all the tables were full of other parents and their unsuspecting children. I had a lemonade and some pickles and then afterward a slice of apple cake.

"Worried about gaining the freshman fifteen?" Grandma patted my knee. "Well, sure. And you're smart to be."

"I'm not worried about that!" I snapped. They were all really getting on my nerves. Couldn't they tell I was going through the most painful day of my existence? And that watching them eat pork while I smelled sauerkraut wasn't helping? Also, seeing all those hot dogs made me miss Oscar, world's strangest dog. And thinking of Oscar made me miss Grant, the only person who understands Oscar. And we were all separated now. Got so upset I had to go into the bathroom and cry for a while. Very embarrassing, because girls who will probably be in my classes kept coming in and there I was sniffling into a paper towel.

Then we were back out, exploring the town. It seemed to me that *all* the stores advertised "Cheese" and "Sausage" and "Bratwurst" in their windows. Like they *wouldn't* have them. Where was the sign for "Organics Sold Here" or "Meat-Free Zone"?

"Grandpa, I *told* you," I had to say before he nearly dragged me into Karl's House of Meat. "I don't eat meat."

"Well, no, not at every meal, of course," Grandpa said.

"Not ever!" Unless you counted the random times I slipped, but those were only 2 or 3 times a year, or maybe a month, at most. Only when I got really stressed out. "How many times do I have to tell you guys? I'm a vegetarian. I'm practically verging on being a vegan."

"A what?" Grandma asked. Her ears turned red. I think she thought I said I was a virgin. Not exactly.

"Nonsense," Grandpa said. "There's no such thing as not eating meat."

I think he has mad-pig disease from all the pork he eats.

"She's just tired from the long drive," Grandma said.

No I'm not! I just want everyone to leave me alone for 2 seconds and quit hovering and let me just cry my eyes out in private, if that's OKAY with everyone.

"Bagle Finagle. What's *that*?" Grandpa turned up his nose as we stopped outside yet another brick building. "Didn't they spell bagel wrong?"

"It's cute," I said, peering inside. To me, it looked like the only cool place in town. It figures that Grandpa wouldn't be able to see that. He was too busy complaining about bagels, and what was wrong with a good old piece of toast, and how toast went so well with bacon and eggs, it was God's food.

I can't *wait* until they all leave tomorrow. I just want classes to start. The sooner classes start, the sooner the semester ends, the sooner I'll be home with Grant.

Did I mention the worst part of the trip?

When we were driving through Nebraska, I saw this evil road sign on the highway: "Exit 126. Ogallala. Grant."

Total conspiracy to make me burst out crying and regret decision to be in a mini-van leaving Grant behind. "They should really put more thought into those signs,"

I told Mom. "It's not very considerate of them."

"It's a town, Courtney," Mom said. "Grant's been here for years and years. It's not a conspiracy."

Sure it isn't. That town's name never *used* to be on the sign, okay?

Then we had to drive through Grant County when we got to Wisconsin. And then I studied the map and realized there is also a Superior, WI, way up north (spent way too much time bonding with AAA maps on the drive). This is in addition to Grant and Superior in Colorado.

Grant Superior is everywhere. Just not here with me, where he should be.

Mom just left, caravanning in Caravan behind Grandpa and Grandma and giant trailer, which Grandma and Grandpa and Mom all slept in last night, in the dorm parking lot. Completely embarrassing when they marched upstairs this morning with towels around their necks, ready for showers. I love her and them. I do. But I was dying for a second of time by myself. All day yesterday, Mom wouldn't stop talking. Probably sensed that I was miserable and was trying to fill the empty, sad aura around my head. Instead she just annoyed me. My aura became irate at one point.

"Look at the trees, Courtney!" Mom kept saying as we drove around. "Have you ever seen anything so beautiful?"

That's Mom. Psyched about the trees, living for foliage, while I'm completely miserable over leaving home.

"These trees are okay, but the aspen back home are more beautiful," I said. "The mountains are beautiful. Living in the same state as my boyfriend is beautiful. *Was* beautiful."

"I know you miss Grant. How about we get some nice, crisp, tart apples and some nice Wisconsin cheddar," she suggested.

How would that fix anything? She *knows* I don't eat cheese. And why did everything have to be so beautiful and *nice* in her world? I was dying inside.

"Mom, *no*," I said. I was talking about the "nice" cheddar, but she thought I was rebuffing her in general and got upset. Then I had to make it up to her by being extra nice the rest of the day. If I were a cheddar, I'd be an extra sharp.

Listen to me! I'm going insane. I have got to drop out of this college immediately. I haven't been in the state for even 48 hours and I'm already using cheese terms to describe myself.

Roommate Alert: Did I mention that Mary Jo got up at 5? On a Sunday? She put headphones on and was listening to music and smiling and reading her bio textbook. Classes haven't even started yet. I haven't even located the *bookstore* yet.

I've got to talk to Grant.

Just tried calling him. Grant is not home. How can he not be home? I need him.

This is going to suck, isn't it?

LATER ...

Just discovered that Mary Jo's mini-fridge is not stocked with soda, as I hoped. The thing is packed full of meat and cheese. It's like a deli case. Filled with meats I don't recognize, like this reddish ham-looking thing with white pieces of something (fat? flesh? bones?) in it. Mary Jo's lucky. If my grandfather had seen this, he would have totally feasted and cleaned the place out.

So I got a glass of water from the drinking fountain.

But you know what? Even the water here tastes like milk. It's like some science fiction universe. A World Made Entirely of Milk. The question is not "Got milk?" but rather, "Got anything *but* milk?" I honestly don't think I can make it here.

Tried to be optimistic. Decided to decorate my side of the room. I put up my animal rights poster. It looks sort of strange next to the picture of Mary Jo from 4-H showing her champion cow Sophie, which is next to the photo of her gold-medal goat Chipper, but, oh well.

Then I hung up my favorite pictures of Grant, and me and Grant. And me and Beth and Jane. And Grant. Pretty soon I had this major collage going, so I finished it.

Then R.A., Krystyne (yes, that's how she spells it), walked by and saw me holding the glue gun. "Uff da!" she yelled.

"Um . . . what?" I said. "Is that a compliment?"

"No, it's Norwegian for 'Whoa, Courtney!'" She started laughing. She was really cracking herself up.

Meanwhile, I was staring at her annoying, red "Cornwall Falls into Your Heart" sweatshirt.

"What did you do? You're not supposed to use that stuff. It's a fire hazard." She said glue wasn't on the list of "approved mounting materials" (what?!). So I had to take down all the photos. She said I had to get a bulletin board, and that they sold some really nice ones at the bookstore.

I was so mad. All the work I'd done. I was just trying

to make this place look like mine. And the pictures were already stuck to the wall; they didn't come off easily. I got so frustrated, I just yanked at one. I ripped in half one of the pictures of me and Grant with our arms around each other.

NOT AN OMEN NOT AN OMEN NOT AN OMEN

I grabbed the Scotch tape and put about 6 layers on. You can't even tell it's me and Grant anymore.

NOT AN OMEN NOT AN OMEN NOT AN OMEN

Need to e-mail Grant now and ask him to send more pictures of us.

LATER STILL . . .

Obviously I will be writing in here constantly, as I am too lonely here and have nothing else to do.

Went into town this afternoon in search of natural foods store, or at the very least some foods more natural than pimento loaf. Mary Jo went to a meeting for the Biology–Chemistry–Pre-med Club. "The program here is incredibly respected," Mary Jo told me before she left.

"So is the political science department," I said. All of a sudden, we were like competing for being smart, discussing GPAs and SAT scores. She got a 780(!!!) on the math part. I immediately changed the subject and told her about my cool work-study job. Which I've got to find more out about tomorrow.

On the way to town, I stopped this guy to ask where

the closest grocery store was. "Take a left at the stop sign," he said. "Then turn right at Hertzmann's Implement."

What? What is an implement? Sounds scary, like something out of a Stephen King novel. Like this whole *experience* so far. *Misery*.

Anyway, when I got to town, I thought I must have fallen asleep and dreamt I was Heidi. These people walked by me on Main Street wearing lederhosen, and the women had their blond hair in cute little wired braids, like Pippi Longstocking.

"*Willkommen!*" one of the men said with this hearty wave.

That's when I realized it wasn't a dream. Oh my God, I thought. What next? I have got to get out of this place.

I found out they were having this festival to celebrate the end of summer, and also to welcome us to campus. They called it the Fall Alpen Fest.

More like Late-Summer Dork Fest. There are no Alps around here, in case no one's noticed. There are a few hills and these things called "mounds" that I read about in Mom's AAA book, but you couldn't ski down one unless you were being towed by a helicopter. Besides, they're sacred, ancient Native American sites, and you shouldn't even be on them, so quit it.

Anyway. Swiss Miss, I'm not. I guess there are lederhosen in my Von Dragen ancestral line, but I'd rather not know about it.

The only people who looked like they were having fun

were the ones in the beer tent, but I wasn't allowed inside since I'm not 21. No all-ages tent anywhere. Completely thoughtless Swiss-German welcome to town.

There was a polka band playing on this little wooden stage that looked more like a gazebo whose walls had blown off. Accordions were flashing in the sunlight. People started to dance. *Oom pah pah* HELP.

I decided I'd sit down and write Grant a letter describing the whole scene. I'd make him laugh, and also realize how lucky he was to still be close to home. I found a spot on the grass that hadn't had mustard spilled on it yet and sat down.

But before I could think of anything brilliant to write to Grant, I noticed this girl sitting a few feet away, writing in a blank book. She was holding a pencil that looked like a whittled tree branch, and her brown hair was tied into about a hundred tiny braids.

She caught me looking at her and she smiled. "Hey, Courtney."

I stared at her. Was I still wearing one of those heinous nametags they'd tried to hand out? No. So how did she know my name? I asked. I'd never seen her before.

"I studied the book," she said. "The freshman book they posted on the website this summer? And I have this photographic memory, so when I saw you I knew. Courtney Smith, Denver, Colorado, Bugling Elk High School."

"Wow," I said, impressed. She was like Raymond in

Rain Man. If I dropped my value-pack of cinnamon Trident she'd probably instantly be able to tell how many pieces were on the ground. "So, um, what's your name?"

"It's time," she said.

"Time?" I said. "For what?" I looked at the stage, wondering if a new polka was about to start up.

"My name. It's time," she said. "T-h-y-m-e. Like the spice? Parsley, sage, rosemary, and me."

"Are those your sisters?" I asked.

"No," she said, laughing. "I was just trying to explain what I meant."

"Oops. *Sorry*," I said. "Thyme's a really cool name." I didn't know anyone with a name like that back home. Well, maybe—there were a Meadow and a Rain in my class. Not to mention a Hope and a Faith. But this is different. This is herbal.

"Yeah, I picked it out myself." Thyme scratched at something on her arm. That's when I realized she didn't shave her underarms. Or her legs.

I really respect that in a woman, but I just can't do it myself. It wouldn't work with my red hair. Also, Mom would have a fit. On top of not shaving, Thyme has about 5 tattoos: 3 on her legs, 1 on her arm, even 1 on her neck. Various goddesses and symbols. Wonder why she doesn't shave, because if she did her tattoos would show up better. But won't mention that until we're closer friends.

I looked around the town square, thinking: if I felt out of place here, how did Thyme feel? Anyway, turns out that Thyme lives 2 doors down, just across the hall. And

19

she and her roommate have already gotten into 3 fights in 2 days.

"Can you believe this cow town? And isn't the dorm a complete nightmare? I can't *wait* until I can move off campus," Thyme said. "Those awful, unhealthy fluorescent lights in the bathroom, plus the hall carpet's made out of like asbestos or dioxin or something—I can't even smell it without sneezing. I mean, it's amazing we're not dead yet."

"Oh, yeah," I said, "I know." I hadn't noticed that yet, but I told myself it's because I've been too upset. "Well, um . . . I like your scarf," I said.

"Thanks! All my clothes are made of natural fibers. Even my shoes."

"Cool." I nodded. Cotton shoes aren't exactly my style, I'm shamefully more of a leather girl, but I did admire her for being so dedicated.

"So anyway, my roommate is like from the Stone Age. She was putting up these shelves for her Treasure Troll collection. Trolls! So I told her I wanted to fung-sway our room, and she was like . . . 'Thyme, what are you talking about?'"

What *was* Thyme talking about? I still don't know.

But she's nice. She's from Chicago, went to an alternative high school, seems interesting. At least I have a lot more in common with her than I do with Mary Jo.

We went off to find the grocery store together. They have some organic vegetables that cost about $3 each and vegetarian baked beans and that's about it. Thyme said since we have to be on the school cafeteria meal plan anyway, and we already paid for that, what we should do is just eat there and scavenge for things that seem remotely healthy.

I told her how I helped get more vegetarian items on the Bugling Elk menu rotation when I was student council VP. She said something about how easy it was to get things done when you "went establishment." Thought it was rude of her to slam me like that, but forgave her when she invited me up to her room to snack on soy-yogurt-covered raisins and nuts. She's probably just stressed out about being here, like I am.

Grant is the best person ever. Best best best best. True to his name. Superior.

He called, and at first it wasn't that much fun. He told me how he likes his roommate, Matt, and how he's sending me pictures of his dorm room and how he got a job at a pet store this afternoon, only it's one of those giant corporate chains—not what he wanted. He went on and on. He sounded so good, so happy . . . I almost really hated him for a minute. How dare he?

Told him I couldn't do this, that I missed him too much and was coming home immediately. That I hated everything here and felt completely out of place.

"Hello? Is this Courtney Von Dragen Smith?" he said, tapping the phone. "Operator? I thought I was talking to Courtney V.D. Smith."

"Will you quit saying that?" I started laughing even though I was still crying. Nobody was allowed to use my middle initials except Grant. "Why are you saying that?"

"Because this isn't you. This really doesn't sound like you."

"The crying part? Or the whining, complaining part?"

"The giving up part. You don't give up that easily. On like, anything."

"I don't?" I asked. Shoot. Because this throwing-in-the-college-towel thing was something I felt I could be a real natural at.

"No." Then he launched into this long laundry list of

things I've pursued that supposedly showed my persever-ance. "And it's one of the things that I really love about you." Grant paused. "Does that help?"

Does it *help*? Grant is like this incredibly hot first-aid kit. When I got back to my room I wrote him a very gushy long letter, which I must take to post office and mail immediately. Perhaps for overnight delivery.

Sweetest thing he has ever done, unless you count the I.D. tag he made for me at Pet Me for Valentine's Day with his phone number on it.

Or the day he called and said he was going to give me a ride to school, but he took me hiking instead.

Or the way he signed my yearbook and wrote "I Love You, Courtney." None of the other boyfriends did that. I took an informal poll. It confirmed what I already knew: Grant is the best boyfriend ever. Superior.

He said it was a zoo the day I left, with everyone showing up to say good-bye to me. "And not the good kind of zoo, either," he said. "The kind where they don't let the animals out."

Not sure what he meant by that. All I remember is pulling out of the driveway in the Caravan. I thought I was going to crumble into a hundred pieces, like those stale egg-less, flour-less muffins they sell at Earthen Fare way beyond their "best if sold by" dates. If they're ever at their best, which I seriously doubt.

I looked at Grant. He looked at me. Mom hit reverse. We nearly knocked over a couple of trash cans because she burst out crying while she was driving.

"Mom, you're not leaving," I said, sobbing. "You get to come back!"

"But—you'll—be—gone," she said, tears almost blinding her from the 4-way stop at the end of our block.

It all seemed so tragic, like I was shipping off to war.

Still and all. A really, really dumb idea to come this far. But it can't be that dumb, because Jane's in Wisconsin, too. And I sort of only agreed to come here because she was leaving home, too, and it seemed like the cool thing to do. Must call her now and compare cheese stories.

LATER . . .

Just had our first official 3rd floor meeting. It was called "The Settling-In Shindig," and was supposedly happening on every floor of every dorm here tonight at the same time. Eerie. Freaky Friday. Except it's Monday.

At the meeting, R.A. Krystyne *actually said* that "Alone" is just "Baloney" without the B and Y! Baloney metaphors. For people in college. *Meat* metaphors. It's like . . . way to make us vegetarians feel welcome. Couldn't she come up with something else? Like: alone is just . . . soybean. Without the s,y,b, and with an l, and if you rearrange all the letters? Sure, it's a lot *harder*. Like everything is if you decide not to eat meat.

She made us all sit in a circle, introduce ourselves, and say something about what we did over the summer and why we chose to come to Cornwall Falls—what influenced our decisions.

"I worked at this smoothie and ice cream café called Truth or Dairy, and I came here due to temporary insanity," were my comments.

Everyone laughed and then Krystyne said, "No, *really*, Courtney."

Really. It's true, I wanted to say. But I came up with something about how I wanted to explore the world beyond in order to better understand the universe. Sounded sort of astronaut-like. Courtney In Space.

Here is my tally so far of the girls on the 3rd floor: Not a complete tally as 3 or 4 girls failed to show for the mandatory meeting. Krystyne went ballistic in a friendly sort of way about that. "Of course it doesn't really matter," she said. "But they definitely ought to be here and there's no acceptable excuse."

- 4 very brainy girls; spent the summer doing very impressive things like working at Wisconsin State Senate and internships at the U.N.; made me feel like a complete idiot
- 3 girls who talked about their boyfriends nonstop; what they did all summer was follow their boyfriends around; they came here because their boyfriends are going here; bluck
- 1 girl who said she came to Cornwall "under duress" because her parents went here and her grandparents went here (hey, I can relate, sister)
- 1 skateboard champion who did tricks on lounge furniture

- 6 girls from the soccer team; we're like the Soccer Block
- 1 girl from Milwaukee
- 1 girl who wouldn't talk, period
- me
- Mary Jo
- Thyme

After we all introduced ourselves, there was a talk from the student health service about not doing drugs and about having safe sex. Like we haven't had the same talk since 6th grade, or 2nd, or whenever it was they started badgering us. (I know it's important and everyone says it can't be said often enough, but trust me, it can.) It went pretty quickly because nobody asked any questions. Nobody *had* any questions.

I caught Thyme's eye a couple of times across the lounge and shook my head. "What are we doing here?" I mouthed.

She rolled her eyes. Later in the talk she interrupted to tell everyone about some new kind of natural-fiber 36-hour tampon that was better for the environment. Everyone looked at her sort of strangely, like you didn't bring up stuff like that in polite conversation. But we were talking about really impolite stuff, like certain types of lubricating gels, so I don't know what their problem was.

Afterward, we all dispersed and went back to our rooms. Which was good because I wanted to finish my package for Grant.

"What are you doing?" Mary Jo asked when I started filling an envelope with a bunch of different things for Grant: a goofy postcard of a cheese factory, a copy of my class schedule, a list of things that seemed weird about Mary Jo. Like the fact she used health and beauty products originally intended for horses or cows. (Grant would probably know all about them: Mane 'n Tail? Udder Butter? Bag Balm? Am I living with a girl or a thoroughbred?) I use stuff not tested on animals. She uses stuff *created for* animals. Which means they have to test it on them, don't they? How can you tell if a horse shampoo is bad, anyway? If its tail has split ends? Who cares?

"I'm putting together a letter for Grant," I told Mary Jo. "My boyfriend, remember?"

"Tell me more about Grant," she said. "What's he like?"

I just sat there and stared at all the pictures of him on the bulletin board. "He's great."

"He's really good-looking," she said. "Are you going to get married?"

"What? I don't know!" I laughed. "How would I know that? I'm only eighteen."

Mary Jo shrugged. "Most people back home know. That's all. My parents got married when *they* were eighteen."

"Oh. Well, see . . . mine didn't," I said. I actually didn't know how old they were, off the top of my head, but I did know they hadn't *stayed* married. Which reminded me. Dad was way behind with his monthly check.

I started writing another letter. *Dear Dad . . . Hello? Do you expect me to live on Saltines and tap water?*

"So, um, do you and Grant have a commitment?" Mary Jo asked. "Like a promise ring?"

I raised my eyebrow. "What? No." I did, however, have the faux rabies tag necklace, which was almost the same thing. And he bought me a new hoop for my belly button, and if that isn't commitment I don't know what is.

"Oh. So you're not serious," Mary Jo said.

"Yes we are!" I protested. What was her problem? "We're *extremely* serious. But we've only been together for about nine months."

Which would mean, if you were my stepsister Angelina, that you'd have a baby by now, but still no commitment.

Getting engaged at 18? I mean, I love Grant and all. But that really hadn't crossed my mind. Should it have? Am I weird for not thinking about it? Does Grant think about it?

So much for cool on-campus work-study job. I was supposed to be a research assistant. I was supposed to be in the law dept. Pictured myself writing legal briefs, wearing suits, appearing in court. Perhaps got a little carried away by watching too much *Law & Order* and *Ally McBeal*. Okay, I admit that. But do I deserve this?

I just called the work-study office to find out about my research-assistant job. The woman on the phone looked up my name, then she sounded nervous and flustered and told me to look in my "welcome packet" for my assignment—I must have missed it.

There was this letter stuffed in there, right underneath the list of Mental Health Resources (which I immediately stashed in my top desk drawer for easy access). It said that due to "changes in funding," my work-study job in the political science/law department had been eliminated.

ELIMINATED. Like something in a James Bond movie.

And it had been replaced by a job in the Cornwall Falls Fun-Times Funders. What is *that*? Sounds like some sort of horrid barbershop quartet. Help me!

LATER ...
Okay, I'm back from the Student Administration building. (Quit administering us already! You're doing a really bad job.)

I now have a job as a glorified telemarketer. Must not tell Mom. She will be furious, since she is obsessed with running all telemarketers out of business, after she settles her lawsuit against the phone company.

Went down to find out what on earth they were talking about. They said my one job had been cut, which was kind of serious because it was lots of hours a week, and this new job was only going to be 5 hours a week. Which is going to amount to like $25 a week at minimum wage, which I can't possibly *live* on, not happily anyway. But they were still giving me all this GRANT money, of course, so not to worry, I should be okey-dokey here at Cornwall Falls. I could either get a job in town. Or I could get loans to make up the rest. Or I could rely on my family's trust fund, or I could start playing the lottery regularly, or I might want to start standing outside the student union, holding an empty coffee can and a placard that says: "Will Take Your Exams for Food."

Okay, those last parts they didn't say.

But the woman I was talking to was acting all bubbly about it, like this was *good* news and I should not be upset.

Excuse me, but that work-study job is part of why I came to this tofu-forsaken town in the first place! I wanted to scream, but didn't, due to the fact there was a line of 50 students behind me. Instead I asked who I should talk to about my assignment. They said I could talk to the Dean of Student Affairs, Dean Robert Sobransky.

I found his office and knocked on the door. In the

catalog, they kept bragging about this "open-door" policy they had when it came to teachers and students. So why was it closed?

He opened the door. Apparently he had just finished getting changed for a tennis match. He asked if he could help me. Which was funny coming from someone wearing too-short white shorts against pale white legs with curly black hair and a bright green polo shirt with the collar turned up. If anything, he needed help. Fashion Emergency.

I introduced myself, calmly. Professionally. Then I went into a slight tirade and said I really had to have an explanation for this. I said I had specifically come to Cornwall Falls because I was promised a chance to work in the law department, and now I find out, after I get here, it's all a ruse, a sham to lure me and innocent other people from Colorado—

"Whoa there, Courtney." He sat on the edge of his desk. "Are you a conspiracy theorist?"

"No, of course not," I said. Though the whole thing was incredibly fishy.

"Good. We have enough of those in our political science department already," he said. "Ha ha ha."

Ha. So hilarious.

He went on to explain that the school learned they had to make budget cuts over the summer, and they cut as few jobs as possible, and I shouldn't take it personally, blah blah blah. . . . But he'd sure be happy to recommend me for anything I found in town, and next semester we

31

could see about getting another work-study job for me, obviously I was in need. I should come talk to him anytime, and if I faced any hardships because of this he'd see what he could do, etc.

The whole time he was talking, he kept tossing a tennis ball up to the ceiling and catching it, over and over, sort of obsessively watching it and trying to get it as close to the ceiling as he could without hitting it. Very weird guy.

"So what is this job I have now?" I finally asked.

He checked out my paperwork and smiled. "You'll be a key member of our Cornwall Falls Funding Team!"

"And that means . . . ?"

"Ah! I keep forgetting you're a freshman," he said. "You seem so much more ma-toor." (That's how he pronounced it.) (What the hell did he mean by that?) (Adults who say this to me always highly suspect.)

"It's in our alumni relations office. You'll be working with our gift programs, contacting alumni, and asking them to donate money, stock, land, what have you."

I guess I must have looked sort of upset, because then he said, "Don't worry, Courtney, I'll work with you every step of the way." At which point he walked into the desk, hit his knee, and started swearing profusely.

Afterward when I left the building, I was so mad I was walking really fast and not paying attention. I crashed right into this kiosk with a million flyers stapled onto it.

There was this girl from my hall standing there, drinking a Mountain Dew and smoking a clove cigarette, and she caught my arm. "Watch out, Courtney!"

"Hey . . . " I said really slowly, as I tried to remember her name. "Annemarie!" She is the one who didn't say a word at our hall meeting except to keep reminding everyone her name was *1 word* and not 2, and her last name was Gustafsen with an e, not an o. She has one of the few single rooms on our hall. Her days so far seem to consist of coming home, slamming her door, putting on loud music like Garbage, Violent Femmes, Beastie Boys. She's never even made eye contact with me, not even in the bathroom when we were both brushing our teeth at neighboring sinks. But now she was actually talking to me. It was so cool.

"You look upset. What's wrong?"

"I just found out my work-study job," I told her. "I have to call alumni and ask them to donate money."

"That sucks. Hey, you know that chick on our hall who doesn't wear deodorant and has that Eve Goddess tattoo? Call her parents," Annemarie said.

"Thyme?" I said. "Why should I call her parents?"

She pointed to a brick building across the quad. "That's theirs. I mean, she told me it's named after them," she said. "The Newell Hall of Economics. Maybe they can cough up some cash for a new dorm and knock ours down."

Thyme's parents are stinking rich? Huh. I'm surprised.

"I could never call former students and ask them for money," Annemarie said. "Aren't we paying this place enough? I mean, I haven't even been here a week and it's like they want eighteen thousand dollars before I can even sign up for my gym card. Not that I want one." She took a drag of her clove cigarette, then offered it to me. "My work-study job is working in the *library*. I can't stand libraries. They're too quiet. I don't know how I ended up here, but I'm transferring."

Annemarie is completely right. I should transfer, too.

Why am *I* here? So I want a degree in environmental law. So my grandfather went here and says it's a great school. Since when have I trusted his opinion? The man thinks pork rinds are a food group. So they came after me and promised me enough financial aid to support me for 4 years and a work-study job. Which they already pretty much took away. Didn't they?

Isn't there more to life? Like . . . a *life*?

Why can't I be getting a scholarship like Grant to study veterinary medicine? Why can't I be any good at the same subjects he is? Grant and I could study side by side. We could open our own practice together. We'd call it Superior Animal Hospital. Brilliant, perfect name.

Except I am afraid of blood. Seeing animals in pain also freaks me out. Could be a problem.

Then I'll be the receptionist. I'll sit in the outer room, away from surgical procedures, and schedule appointments on environmentally friendly 100 percent recycled paper without thinking too long about what they're for. I'll be oblivious. Negligent. Whatever.

Mary Jo and I are *not* getting along.

I was getting dressed this morning and all of a sudden Mary Jo shrieked and said, "What's that on your stomach? Oh my God!"

She was referring to my pierced navel.

I explained that this was a piece of jewelry. She still seemed really confused about the whole thing.

"Well, I just think that's, um, I don't know. Wrong?"

"What's wrong about it? People pierce their ears. And lots of other things," I reminded her.

"Yeah, but—I don't know. It makes me think of the way that our cows have to get tags stapled to their ears to tell them apart," Mary Jo said.

She was comparing my navel to a cow's ear?

"Yeah, but that probably hurts them," I said. "This didn't." Not much, anyway. Except for the way it swelled up whenever I didn't use enough Hibiclens on it. "And besides, I *chose* to mutilate myself. I mean decorate myself. Whatever. Cows don't have that choice." Ha! So there for getting all self-righteous on me. At least I never stapled a cow.

Maybe people argue so much here because of the crappy weather. It's so hot. There's like 97 percent humidity. My hair is a frizz pile. Rain came in through the window and soaked the granola fruit bars I left on the windowsill, and now they're oatmeal. All the photos on my bulletin board are curled up at the corners. My towel smells like mildew. *I* smell like mildew.

"This is nothing," Mary Jo said. "Last spring it rained so much, our basement flooded. And outside? The cows kept falling in the mud and a couple of them broke their legs."

"How long is this going to last? I really need some sun," I said.

"Don't worry, Courtney—you'll get used to it," Mary Jo told me when I kept staring out the window.

"I don't *want* to get used to it," I said. "I want to get away from it. The weather back home is so much better."

Mary Jo got insulted and left for the cafeteria without waiting for me or anyone else. Like she's responsible for the rain?

LATER ...

Back from my new, exciting job.

Had to phone people today and remind them what a great place "Cornball" Falls is.

Hello? Does anyone see a problem here?

So far I haven't even been here a week, and I hate it. But there I was with my canned lines, reading them off a script that's so worn it looks as if it's been used by students every year since 1915.

"Your donation provides valuable support for students like me."

"Would you consider increasing your gift this year?"

"Would you like to donate a building?"

"Would you like fries with that?"

There's this ear-of-corn Velcro poster-thing on the wall that measures how well we're doing on the fund drive, like a thermometer filled with corn kernels instead of mercury. It looks like a project for a day-care center. And everyone has these signs up on their cubicle walls in front of them, to prod them into pushing for more money, like a reward system. "Way to Go, Rachel! $250!" and "$1,000—You Rule, Wittenauer!" Those are for the upperclassmen.

And then there's me. "Courtney. Keep Improving. $20."

Hey, is it my fault I get the losers' cards?

We have these index cards we have to use for each alum, with all this personal info, like what dorm they lived in, and what their major was, and what they do now, and how many kids they have. We have weekly goals, total amounts. So far I'm several hundred dollars short. Okay, thousands. I know—I'll flip through the cards, find the person with the largest donation ever, hit them up. Is there a chance in hell that Bill Gates went to Cornball Falls?

This afternoon was fun. Thyme and I went to the bagel place for coffee. I asked her about the Newell Hall of Economics. She launched into their entire family history. "It's—it's not my dad, it was my grandfather, because he went here," she said.

Are we all just here because of grandparents? *Must* we pay for their generation's mistakes?

Her grandfather gave the money a long time ago when he made a ton of money by inventing something or other. Then he got pushed out of the company, and Thyme said he was "a victim of evil downsizing corporate warfare." Is that typical or what? So they did have a lot of money, but they don't anymore. How sad. Whereas I don't have any money now, and never really had any, although I did all right working at T or D.

After coffee we went to the bank so I could open an account with my last few paychecks. Thyme already had an account but she came with me. Which was funny, because there were all these signs all over the bank: "Tyme is money," plastered on the cash machines. Turns out Tyme is the name of the ATM network here. I asked Thyme if that was embarrassing and she said she liked the juxtaposition of a free spirit and a corporate establishment. "Because it's so untrue, you know. Me, Thyme? I'm not money. I'm so *anti*-money. So it's so ironic."

The customer service person totally gave me the 3rd degree. She made me fill out a dozen forms, sign in 18 places. She practically wanted a sample of my blood. She was so suspicious of me, it was ridiculous. I was going to leave and open an account at another bank, but I'd filled out so many forms I felt like I couldn't move.

"Von . . . what does that say? Van Dragon?" the woman asked.

"Your middle initials are V.D.?" Thyme asked. "Ooh. How rude."

"Tell me about it," I said.

"It's better than STD though. I guess." Thyme started laughing, and then told me if I thought my middle name was bad, *hers* was Penelope. So I guess things could be worse. Maybe. Thyme Penelope equals T.P. Not good at all.

I got this big lecture on how not to bounce checks and customer service woman said they had problems with new students every fall, blah blah blah, and she hoped they wouldn't have trouble with *me*, Courtney Von Dragoon Smith. Like we're small children and can't take care of ourselves or something without *her* telling us how to add and subtract? It was so insulting.

"I've never bounced a check in my life," I said.

She smiled, sort of. "Oh, I'm sure you haven't, Ms. Smith. But if you have, we'll find out about it."

"What a witch," I said to Thyme as we left. "She's out to get me or something."

"It's clear-cut ageism," Thyme agreed. "You could file a complaint. *I* would."

"Maybe I should switch banks," I said.

"Don't bother. They're all the same." Thyme flipped her skinny braids over her shoulder. "I don't even believe in banks, but they're a necessary evil."

"Like coffee?" I joked.

We laughed and went over to the student center for another 3 cups. After that we were so wired we went to gym to work out. Thyme did yoga; I sprinted on LifeCycle. Felt like a real athlete until actual cycling club walked into gym. Very fit. Sleek. Me, sweating out coffee, face red from exertion. Thyme walked up cool and refreshed from basically lying on foam pad for an hour. Guys in club checked her out, ignored me.

Must give up coffee. Must also invest in sleeker workout clothes.

I got a package from Grant!!! Yes! Good karma, because I tried so hard today to get settled here. I went to classes and bought my books.

Inside Grant's package was a Colorado State notebook and baseball cap. Plus an old T-shirt of his I'd been pestering him for. I'm putting it in my book bag and carrying it everywhere and when I miss him, I'll take it out and smell it.

People will look at me strangely, but I don't care. They probably already do, because I'm not Norwegian or Swedish or whatever everyone is here. (I'm not tall, I'm not blond. What am I, anyway?) (Too philosophical a question for me right now.)

Grant's package gave me a burst of energy, and then I realized how much I miss him and started to cry. Why didn't I go to CSU? What's wrong with me? Why do I make such bad choices?

I needed to calm myself. If I were back home, I'd drive to the buffalo overlook and check out the herd. But no such luck. No buffalo here. No car.

But we are out in the country, and it was actually a sunny afternoon, so I got on my bike, hoped it wouldn't rain, and rode out of town. The road I was on was curvy and pretty. Not to mention bumpy. Green trees, wildflowers everywhere. Reminded me of a picture in the CF catalog. The one they used to shamelessly lure me here.

Anyway, there I was, riding on scenic country road,

feeling really happy for once, except for constant rolling hills that all went straight up, and the fact I'm not in the best shape of my life. Then I went past this sign that said BUCK'S TAXIDERMY—i.e., e.g., turning dead animals into living statues/monuments to hunting skill. Then beneath the "Buck's" part, like I wasn't getting a graphic enough picture of exactly what he was talking about, the sign said FUR, FOWL, ETC.

"Etc."? What does that mean? People? Reptiles? Swine? Disgusting.

When I got to the cows, they were marching single file along this path to the barn. I put down my bike and walked over to look at them. They were so orderly, they looked like soldiers. Milk soldiers. Fighting for dairy. Fighting for their lives, no doubt. Do dairy cows get to retire to green(er) pastures? Or when they're milked out, are they turned into burgers? Poor cows. They'd be cute if they weren't full of gallons of milk.

I went back to my bike and realized I'd set it down in world's largest cow chip. Spent an hour scraping off the seat with a stick. Bluck.

My first "real" weekend here, without relatives! Yes!

There was a major catastrophe here this morning: everyone realized there was no home football game and no home *anything* games this weekend. Girls (except soccer players who were at practice) drifted aimlessly until everyone paired off into different cars to head to the outlet mall.

Okay, not everyone. Annemarie stayed in dorm, music blaring. Mary Jo got irritated and went to science library so she could study in peace and quiet. Thyme went on hike with CF Nature Club. Kept trying to convince me to go with her, but I couldn't.

Last night I figured out I have to get a job in town right away. My money is running out very quickly.

Job search really sucked. Everything's already taken, or I'm not qualified, or I don't *want* to dress up like Helga and wear horns on my head and serve German potato salad on roller skates at the Vivacious Viking.

For some reason in this town, employers only want kids who are 14 and 15 to scoop ice cream. Even though it's totally clear I have the muscle for it from working at T or D and could outscoop them, *plus* I know about smoothies and wheatgrass, which they're going to have to make the transition to sometime. But no. Looked at me as if I were speaking foreign language.

Plus half of the places served frozen custard, and I don't even know what that is. Who eats frozen pudding?

I thought that was like . . . British or something. Or is that flan? What *is* flan?

There are the 6 or 7 identical-looking souvenir shops, where you can buy trolls, German beer steins, and any Cornwall Falls College T-shirt your heart desires. (Which would be none, so far.) In one of the stores, this man kept offering me fudge and cheese samples. In another, the women working there kept giving me dirty looks, like I was going to steal a bronzed badger or a cuckoo clock or something. No thank you. I have enough crap in my room, thanks to Mary Jo.

I was sitting outside on the brick wall by the dorm, thinking about whether there was a plasma bank nearby, whether I could finance my higher education *that* way, or maybe an egg bank, after all I'm in the prime of my reproductive life, aren't I? And aren't you supposed to be able to get a few thousand bucks for some prime eggs? I've got several dozen to spare.

I had totally given up hope when Tricia came by. She's the bubbly one who said during our drugs 'n' sex talk that she'd organized a rally to keep *every single kid in her neighborhood* off crack, and it worked, gosh darn it.

Like they have crack in Walla Walla, Idaho, or whatever small town she said she was from. Like they even have neighborhoods.

"Courtney! What are you *doing* up there?" she asked. As if no one had ever sat on a wall before. She had this giant pink Cornwall sweatshirt on and a matching hair ribbon. Her hair is the color of corn, just like Mary Jo's, but also has many, many faux shiny highlights. If this place had sororities she'd be all over them. But that's one of the reasons I liked this place—or thought I liked this place, anyway—no exclusive Greek societies. No "rushing," except maybe to class when I'm late because I'm riding my bike through snowdrifts.

Anyway, I told Tricia how I have to find a job, and she excitedly started shrieking how the place where she worked was hiring. "Um, and where's that?" I asked, expecting her to say the Hallmark store. Which wouldn't be so bad, actually, because I'll be buying lots of cards this year to send to Grant.

"Bagle Finagle!" she said. "It's so cool, and so fun. And I know Jennifer would hire you in a second? Because she's the manager? And she's really cool?" Tricia says everything like a question.

I thought about what Gerry said to me on my last day of work at T or D as he toasted me with a Coconut Fantasy Supreme. "Any employer would be lucky to have you. But don't bowl them over with your individuality." Whatever *that* meant.

So she took me over there and I filled out an application. Everyone working there seems nice. Jennifer seems sort of like a tyrant, but who cares? I need money.

"It would be so great if we could get the same shifts?" Tricia said after we left to walk back to the dorm together.

"Um . . . yeah," I said, thinking, *Um, no. Not really. Not at all, actually.* She would probably try to organize a rally to keep me off caffeine.

Very funny thing happened this morning for brunch. We were all traipsing off to the cafeteria together, en masse, that's how we've been doing everything. (Is the 3rd floor hungry? Does the 3rd floor need to go to the post office? We must do everything in groups of no less than 15.)

So we were going down the stairs and I was between Mary Jo and Thyme. Mary Jo was asking Thyme about her tattoos and how much it hurt to get a tattoo. Girl is obsessed with pain of body art—why? Is she considering getting Sophie memorialized? Where?

"Well, MJ," Thyme said. She paused. "Is it okay if I call you MJ?"

"Um, well . . . " Mary Jo tried to be polite at first.

"Well, MJ, the thing about tattoos is—"

"Please, um, don't . . . call me MJ," Mary Jo said.

"Oh? But it's so natural. And it's sort of more, you know, twenty-first century, when you think about it—"

"Not really. And besides, nobody calls me that."

"But it could be a nickname—"

"*No*," Mary Jo said. "It couldn't." Then she moved ahead and started walking next to other people. Completely blowing us off!!!

Surprising amount of backbone considering everyone has been doing everything humanly possible just to get along for the past 4 days and has been clinging to each other like the way we desperately grasp trays in the cafeteria. Not me. Of course. Them.

LATER—GREAT NEWS!

I got the job!!! Yes!!! I'll make $6.75 an hour plus get 2 free bagels with every shift (toppings not included, but who needs toppings?). No need to waste time at horrid cafeteria eating oyster crackers for lunch anymore.

First I called Beth. She was hungover, but very happy for me. Then I called Grant. He was out so I left a hyper message on his answering machine. His roommate's voice is on the machine, which bugs me, because I want to at least hear Grant saying he isn't home. It's so unsatisfying to call and not hear him say *anything*.

Then I called Mom but she wasn't home, so I talked to Bryan. He said he was doing okay in cross-country. I knew that was an understatement because Mom told me the newspaper did a big article on him. When you talk to him, though, he doesn't mention it. Nothing about paces, or splits, or meets he's won by a minute. I asked if he was hungover, too, like Beth. He said no. He said she's been going kind of wild and was going to parties every night of the week.

Somehow that didn't sound too good to me. I don't know why, I mean, I know I've only been gone for a week so things can't have changed too much. Maybe I'm just jealous. So far I haven't been to any parties. Thyme and I went to the movies last night. Afterward we went to this little café near campus and drank herbal tea. Which sounds like something Grandma would do with *her* friends.

Question: What is it like for Thyme to drink thyme tea?

Anyway, went across hall to tell Thyme about my new job. She was sort of happy at first, but then she got this glum look.

"Have you checked into their investments?" she asked. "I think I heard they get their flour from some country that's on an Amnesty International watch list. And aren't they owned by some major oil corporation?"

"Um, I don't know," I said. "I think they just have stores in the upper Midwest."

"Yeah, okay. But you should really check out their investment background."

"Sure, of course," I said. But if the place is good enough for her to buy coffee from, isn't it okay for me to work there? I mean, if you're going to boycott a place, you have to be a *little* more consistent.

"I get free bagels, so you know, if you ever want some, just come by during my shift," I offered.

"I can't. Bagels plague my harmonic system," she said.

Okay. Whatever. You're welcome.

Fortunately Mary Jo knocked on the door then, looking for me. Grant was on the phone. Yes! Spent an hour talking to him. The whole time, Mary Jo was getting ready for bed, then going off to brush her teeth with her little horse-product bucket (horse toothpaste?), and then she came back, and then she was reading in bed, and then she turned out her light, etc.

When I got off the phone, she said, "I really don't want to make a big deal out of this. But do you think you could maybe call Grant, like, during the day sometimes?"

What? "It's pretty hard. It's expensive during the day, plus he has class, and then he works, and—anyway, I didn't call him. He called *me*."

"It's just that my schedule this semester is going to be really hard," Mary Jo said. "I'm sorry."

So then I had to feel like a real jerk. "No, I'm sorry," I said. "I'll try not to be on the phone so late." But if Grant calls? I am not *not* going to talk to him.

I wish Beth were my roommate, not Mary Jo. Beth would be *fun*. We'd stay up late, listen to good music, fridge would be stocked with Frappuccinos and fresh-squeezed juice; we'd probably even buy a juicer and share it. Maybe she wants to transfer. No, wait. I want to transfer.

My training for Bagle Finagle was tonight from 5–8. 3 long hours involving history of company, history of bagels, history of flour and cream cheese. Yawn.

"We have fifty-six Bagle Finagles across the upper Midwest, and we're rising like dough!" Jennifer is definitely a little on the annoying side. Okay, a lot. There were 9 other people in training, but after we took a bathroom break there were only 5 of us left. 1 was this very funny guy named Mark, a freshperson like me, who wore 3 earrings in one ear, had a bleached crewcut, and club look.

They're introducing some new bakery items, so Jennifer gave us each samples. There was a cinnamon roll with inch-high frosting, and something called the Muller's Cruller, which looked like a hot dog bun that had fallen into a vat of glue.

"Who the hell is Muller?" one guy asked.

Mark nudged me and said, "Check this thing out. It's like glazed to within an inch of its life." He took a bite, then tossed the rest into the trash can. It made such a loud clang that we cracked up laughing and then got a dirty look from Jennifer. She does that a lot. Glares at people.

I kept staring at this obnoxious sign by the cash register (right under the giant NO CHECKS sign; people are obsessed with bad checks in this town, there are signs at every cash register I've seen so far):

OUR NAME MIGHT BE BAGLE FINAGLE, BUT DON'T FINAGLE THE BAGELS! There was a set of handcuffs hanging down, like they'd actually handcuff someone for stealing a bagel? Maybe they save those for the more violent crimes. Like stealing scallion-chive cream cheese.

Speaking of cheese. What is their number-one seller? Cheese bagels. With cheddar-cheese-flavored cream cheese. Bluck.

There are regulations regarding how to stack napkins on the counter so the logo always faces out. We had tests regarding how many ounces of cream cheese make up a slather, and how many make up a super slather. If a customer asks for extra pickles on their bagel sandwich, they get 2 more than standard. Personal phone calls can last only 30 seconds. Etc. Mark asked about smoke breaks and that started a whole debate about whether the rest of us should get breaks even though we don't smoke, and then 1 more girl quit because she said she didn't want to work with anyone who smoked, period.

"Give me a break," Mark said. "Does she think I'm going to blow secondhand smoke in her face? Well, who cares. I'm glad she's gone, because *I* don't want to work with anyone who wears a Packers T-shirt."

I asked Mark how he felt about wearing the goofy BF aprons. He said he'd find a way to make it work for him. "Or I'll find a way to work it," he said. "Period."

Jennifer overheard us and asked Mark what he meant by that, and then reminded us about the strict dress and hair codes.

I thought about Gerry wanting to start a little chain of his ice cream and smoothie shops. So far he has 2 locations for Truth or Dairy. Really on a roll there.

But maybe Gerry has the right idea. This place is a bit on the rigid side. No room for individualism or self-expression. In other words, you have to ask the same questions in the same tone of every single customer. The first one is the killer. I can't picture these words coming out of my mouth, but I guess they will: "What kind of bagel can I finagle for you?"

And if I can say that without dying of embarrassment, I get to run through the "Option Board": "Sliced? Toasted? Would you like cream cheese with that? Anything to drink with that? Would you like to make this a steal deal?" Why do I sound like a Fembot? Ugh. But this won't be so bad. From wheatgrass juice to wheat 'n' honey bagels. Same healthy principle, but better tasting.

When I got back to the dorm I was feeling very outgoing as a result of our "Bagle-Bonding" exercises. We each had to pretend to fall into a boiling vat of water and have our team catch us, also did the same thing pretending to fall into the oven. Seemed sort of sadistic or at the very least a rip-off of "Hansel and Gretel." I stopped by Thyme's room to see if she wanted to go out. She told me how she finally feng-shui-ed the room, and then she showed me a book on feng shui, so now I know what she's talking about.

We went to the student center. It was really dead, not surprising because it is Monday night. Ended up going into the pool hall/video game/bowling alley area. Neither of us is very good at pool, but we met some guys who kept challenging us to another game, even though they kept winning.

I had an okay time, but Thyme was annoyed because they kept making fun of her name. First they compared her to the Tyme machine on the wall and kept calling her "Money." Then, when that got old, they started calling us "Parsley" and "Sage" and saying things like, "Hey, Rosemary, it's your turn," and humming that Simon & Garfunkel song about the spices.

"People are so closed-minded," she muttered on our way back to the dorm. "Haven't they ever heard of originality? Haven't they ever heard of being an individual? They were so paternalistic and *standardized*."

I don't know. I thought they were actually sort of fun. Reminded me of guys from home. Like Grant. Sigh. Only 10.5 weeks until Thanksgiving.

Sitting in student center with Thyme. Since neither one of us really loves being in our rooms, this is like our home now. She's using photographic memory to help me memorize everything for my first shift tomorrow at BF. We get an actual report written up with things we need to work on. I hate those kind of reports. I've hated "Needs Improvement" since kindergarten.

The thing is that Thyme should be the one who goes to work at BF because she's looked at the setup there all of *once* and has it down cold. She has even drawn me a map of all the bagel bins. This is something I could hate her for if she weren't so nice about it. But nice in a condescending way, because she doesn't understand what it's like to have faulty, real-time memory and confuse sesame seed with poppy seed.

Anyway, we were sitting there drinking coffee and working on this when Tricia came by. She said it was a really good idea for me to be so prepared? And that she'd mention it to Jennifer? She said that Jennifer was this incredibly wonderful manager who might insist on the rules a lot? But was only doing that for our benefit, and I shouldn't take it personally if she yelled at me; she yelled at everyone?

Great. I am so looking forward to my first day.

Scored big points on several levels today. I'd celebrate but I have a ton of homework to do.

Spoke up in my sociology class.

Actually got someone to donate some money tonight. Thank you, Mrs. Benson of Chippewa Falls, for increasing your gift this year. No thank you for the long story detailing the history of the grain elevator.

This morning, aced my first shift at BF. Mostly because of coworker named Ben. Incredibly nice, English major, sophomore, fishitarian. He took about 90 percent of the orders and let me work slowly until I got things straight.

I asked all the right preformulated questions, didn't mess up the cream cheese types. One error, though: forgot my hairnet. Okay, pretended to forget it. Was hoping no one would notice. Jennifer scolded me. I put it on and as soon as I did, who walked in but the one cute guy who came in all day.

Not that I care what random guy thinks, but still. Felt like lunch lady about to dish up Sloppy Joes. Need cat-eye glasses on a chain to complete the look.

Went online to do research for my poli sci paper tonight. After Mary Jo *finally* finished writing her paper and got off the computer. So rude. I had so much work of my own to do, and she really should be using the computer lab, only I'm so nice I offered to let her use my computer because she wasn't feeling very well. Well, who *would* if they insisted on eating the cafeteria's all-beef chili?

Ended up getting 9 Tarot card readings, 6 different horoscopes, and spent 2 hours in an LDR chat room. Everyone was pouring out their tales of woe. There were like 5 people out of 100 who said they'd managed to make it work.

"Agree to see other people" was the major advice. There were also a lot of angry "It'll never work!" comments and "You'll break up," so "See other people." I know it was all coming from guys. I could just tell. But after I read all that, I couldn't concentrate. I kept wondering if Grant thought anything like that. I e-mailed Grant, but he didn't write back within a few minutes. Called Grant. Not home. Left message. Then Mary Jo asked me to please be quiet. It's 9:30!!!

This *isn't* going to work.

Thank God tomorrow's the last day of August. Almost September, but that's not good enough. Please let it be October soon, so we'll be closer to November and Thanksgiving and me going home or at least getting out of here for a few days.

Can't believe what happened today. I'm writing this in the first-floor lounge while other people watch TV because I can't be in my room right now. I'm not welcome. Also it just feels really really awkward and uncomfortable. Maybe it's all my fault, but I don't think so.

Thyme and I had this brilliant insight over lunch, as we surveyed the salad bar for edibles: The Great Roommate Switch. It would be so easy for me just to move across the hall. And Mary Jo and Kirsten get along as well as Thyme and I do, right?

So we went to the housing office to plead our case. We immediately got to see 2 housing counselors. But they wouldn't even "entertain" the idea. I pointed out how different me and Mary Jo are, and how they were supposed to match us with someone compatible. Not someone who eats rolled slices of ham and Swiss for breakfast.

They said that part of college was learning people skills and how to get along with others who were different. They said they'd evaluated all the applications with "personal growth" in mind. And anyway, the semester was already 2 weeks old, they'd done their best, and there was nothing they could do about it now. Thyme started going on a rant about how she was being forced to listen to pop music and it was stunting her personal growth. But it didn't help. Actually, I think she sort of hurt our cause. We left feeling utterly defeated.

So we walk out to the front desk, and who's standing there, waiting to talk to the same counselors? MARY JO AND KIRSTEN!!! How rude. I mean, it's one thing for me and Thyme to want to switch. We have *reasons*.

So we all got really embarrassed and uncomfortable and everyone started mumbling about how we were just reporting the fact that the showers need more water pressure, and how there's this girl on our floor who's drunk every night and we're very concerned about her, etc.

Does Mary Jo hate me that much? What's up with that? Am I so hard to live with? My family never had a problem with me.

Entire hall went to big pro–Cornwall Falls rally tonight. Mary Jo and Kirsten were hovering together, avoiding me and Thyme. Like Thyme and I wanted to hang out with them. Like we wanted to even go to the rally. But Krystyne insisted that this was a fun, all-campus event and we'd be sorry if we missed our first one, and of course she couldn't force anyone, but it would look really bad and it wouldn't be "in the spirit of team spirit"—

At which point Annemarie slammed the door in her face and turned up the new Green Day CD.

Thyme and I went to the rally for about 3 minutes, then ditched it. Thyme insisted on going to a workers' rights rally outside the student center instead. Only about 20 people there. Couldn't hear the speaker because the marching band was blaring jock hits of the 1980s and the crowd was singing/yelling along. Also, we were downwind from the big bonfire. Smoke kept getting in my eyes and making me cough.

Go Cornwall Falls, though. Really. Win win win.

"You should have come," Mary Jo said, when we met up back at the room.

For once I think maybe she was right about something.

Got off work at noon. Had to be there at 6 to open. Grueling. Anyway, turned out to be fun, because I got to work with Mark and Ben (and also Tricia, who we assigned to be money finagler and therefore got to mostly ignore all morning). Place was really crowded, but we handled it. When we were getting off work, Ben asked me whether I was going to the big football game. I told him that I had other plans. "Oh, well, that's cool. What are your plans?" he asked.

"Um, well, I was thinking of maybe, um, reading," I said. "Either that or sitting around missing my boyfriend."

"Are you insane? Come on, you've got to go to the game. Everyone goes. You can't call yourself a Cornwaller Faller until you do."

"And I'd *want* to call myself that?" I asked.

He laughed. Somehow, 5 minutes later, Ben, Mark, and I were heading over to the field. I didn't think I should go because Thyme and I pledged we'd never do anything as stupid as attend a football game. Even though I did it a lot in high school, that was a long time ago. I'm older now. More mature. "Besides, the human violence that game promotes is just unthinkable," Thyme said, and she's right, helmets bashing, concussions and separated shoulders all over the field. She was going to spend the day searching for wildflowers and then collecting evidence of harmful chemicals in the dorm drinking water.

So Mark, Ben, and I got there and the game had already started. It was true: everyone was there, and it didn't seem to have much to do with the actual game. I heard someone yelling my name and looked up in the bleachers and saw a bunch of girls from my floor sitting in a row. Mary Jo was waving at me and gesturing for me to come join her. I waved back. I felt important for a second, being recognized. "My roommate," I explained to Mark and Ben. "My whole *floor*, actually."

"Who's the leather chick?" Mark asked. "I dig her."

I couldn't believe it. Annemarie was sitting next to Krystyne and wearing her black motorcycle jacket. She had probably been dragged there, under duress. She had her Walkman on. I was explaining her to Mark when there was some big play on the field, and Cornwall Falls got the ball. All of a sudden the cheerleaders, who had been sitting in front of us, sprang to their feet. They started chanting the school's initials and thrusting their arms into the air.

"C—F—C! C—F—C!"

It sounded so familiar. Then, for the first time ever, it dawned on me. I stared at their sweaters, at the guy cheerleader's megaphones. CFC. It's not just Cornwall Falls College. It's chlorofluorocarbon. It's a harmful chemical. It's been *banned* because it's responsible for the destruction of the ozone layer. And this is the school I ended up at? And they have the nerve to stand around and *chant* that—like it's a good thing?

A running back got knocked out of bounds just then

and nearly knocked us down, so we had to move. I ended up sitting with Ben and some of his friends for a while, then at halftime went to sit with Annemarie, who kept making me wear her headphones to check out new songs, which was more fun than listening to people chant "C—F—C." At one point I could have sworn I saw Thyme sitting across field in opposing team bleachers.

"Is that Thyme over there?" I asked.

Annemarie laughed. "Are you *high*? If she was here, it would be because she was organizing a protest for cheerleaders' rights or the exploitation of hot dog vendors."

"True," I said. "Well, they *are* exploited. The cheerleaders, I mean. But I can think of a few things I'd rather protest." I was talking for a while before I realized Annemarie had her headphones back on and wasn't listening to me anymore. Rest of crowd was on its feet cheering wildly for C—F—C.

Very embarrassing moment today in front of entire college. Might need to think about transferring sooner than planned.

There was this big party outside on the quad today—the Fall Semester Kickoff. It didn't rain. Amazing. Unheard of. There were 3 bands that played, plus a giant cookout, corn on the cob, etc. Thyme and I started out sitting with everyone on our hall, but after a while took off to wander around and check out the crowd. Everyone was in a really good mood. I was having fun. We went out and started dancing.

Then I thought I heard someone calling my name. I had no idea who it would be—thought maybe it was Mark. I kept looking around while I danced. The music got softer and I realized it wasn't just one person shouting my name, it was several. "Courtney, Courtney!"

What? I was thinking. I'm not *that* good—or bad—of a dancer. And I only know like *12* people here.

"Courtney, Courtney!"

So I yelled, "What?"

Then I heard a bunch of people laughing. Someone tapped me on the shoulder, someone with really long hair that tickled my neck. I turned around.

That's when I saw the giant cob of corn dancing behind me.

First I thought there must have been drugs in the brownies I'd just eaten. Then I realized they weren't yelling "Courtney" at all, they were yelling "Corny!" Because I was standing face-to-face with *Corny*, the Cornwall Falls mascot. An ear of corn. With long, fake blond hair sticking out of its neck, a giant yellow helmet, a bright green peeling-off costume on its body.

He/she/it took my hand and started twirling me around.

Why are school mascots drawn to me? Why? I was mauled by the Bugling Elk in high school, and in middle school I was kissed by some guy in a tiger suit from the opposing team.

Is it because I love animals so much, that people who dress up as animals feel this overpowering need to get close to me? But wait. That doesn't explain Corny guy. Unless vegetables can feel the love?

"Hey, how's it going?" he said.

"Come on, Thyme. Let's go," I said.

"Cool. We can get back to the dorm in time for that PBS special on communism," Thyme said.

That wasn't exactly my idea of alternative fun, but, oh, well. Maybe now I can skip that chapter in my poli sci textbook.

Spent all morning on the phone with Grant. Mary Jo was off at her 9:10 class and then her 10:10 and after that I lost track. It was great to have the room to myself. Of course it meant that I missed my 11:10, but, oh, well.

Anyway, I told Grant all about my weekend. He said it sounded like fun.

"Grant, I think we're growing apart," I said.

"What?" He sounded panicked. "What do you mean by that?"

"It wasn't fun. It was awful."

"Oh. Well, okay." He laughed. "In that case, my weekend was awful, too."

"What did *you* mean by that?" I asked.

I was worried that we weren't communicating very well. First sign of trouble, according to everyone in LDR chat room.

But then our conversation went on for 2 more hours and involved many goofy romantic comments, so I think we're okay. Not to worry. Grant loves me. I love Grant. I can't wait to see him at Thanksgiving, even if it must be at Grandma and Grandpa's in Nebraska, surrounded by relatives and turkeys.

Is that redundant?

We haven't figured out the plan yet, but he might hitch a ride with Mom and Bryan just so he can see me. Hurrah!

Made major gaffe today at work. It was a slow time and I was studying the sandwich cards. I still don't have them all memorized and I hate looking stupid and checking the cards when people come in, and if I *don't* get them right, Jennifer gets mad. So anyway, Ben and I were talking about what an adjustment it was, living in a small town like Wauzataukie, going to what he calls "Cowpie Falls." We were joking about the Cornwall Falls and how we've never actually *seen* the falls, and maybe it's just another catalog ruse to get people to campus. And how it would be nice to have at least one place where we could buy clothes we liked.

"So where do you get your clothes?" I asked. Because they were very cool, except of course for the standard BF apron.

"On line," he said. "You know, you could order your whole life on line if you needed to."

"Really? There's a website for that?" I asked. "Give me a password. Like, now."

Ben laughed. "It's definitely weird being here," he said. "I mean, I feel like such an outsider."

"Oh, I know!" I said. "I *totally* understand." (Only I didn't.)

"You do?" Ben asked.

"Sure. I'm from Colorado and nobody really gets that. I mean, they don't even really know where that *is*. Half the people here can't find it on a map."

Ben looked a little confused, like we weren't having the same conversation anymore. He took off his gold-wire glasses and rubbed a spot off them. "Okay, but you couldn't tell the difference between Illinois and Indiana the other day," he reminded me. Jennifer had quizzed us on other Bagle Finagle locations, because that's the kind of thing she does for fun.

"That's different—they're smaller and they both start with I. But who confuses Colorado and Wyoming?" I asked. "Anyway, everyone just thinks that all I ever did was *ski* all day, and they expect me to be a certain way, and they expect me to know what a hot dish is, and they expect me to love meat and cheese and milk and have blond hair, and I just *don't*."

Ben looked at me and sighed. "Courtney, I'm sure that's sort of frustrating and all. But actually, I was talking about being African-American? And how we're only like five percent of the student population?"

"Oh." I felt like *such* an idiot. "Sorry," I said. I couldn't apologize enough. I think I said it 100 times.

"It's okay, you didn't know," Ben said.

"Well, I did kind of have an idea," I said.

Then we both cracked up laughing. Ended on a good note. But still. How insulting was that, talking about *skiing* and not being Scandinavian?

I think I probably have overestimated how hard this is for me. It's probably much harder for other people. I'm probably being self-involved to the point of absurdity. All I really have to deal with is a lack of sun, mild heartbreak, and 5,000-foot altitude change. If I can't handle that, then I'm really pathetic. But then I knew that already, sort of.

Must make a bigger and better effort to get settled here. Must find groups to join. But then I think of that Groucho Marx line that Woody Allen quotes at the beginning of *Annie Hall*, Mom's favorite movie, about never wanting to belong to a club that would have me as a member. And what sort of club could I join, anyway?

I realized the big benefit of my dumb work-study job today. Am I that dense that Annemarie had to point it out to me? *Free long distance*.

First I called Jane to invite her up for this weekend, next weekend, any weekend. She has a car and I don't, but then she lives in a cool place—Madison—and I don't, so who knows when we'll actually get together. Besides, she has a new boyfriend, someone in a band who is writing songs about her already. I want Jane's life.

Then I called Beth, but she was too busy at work to talk.

Then I called Grant, totally thinking he wouldn't be home, was just going to leave a message. But he was *there*! I was complaining about feeling so left out and Grant gave me some great advice.

"Courtney, look. If you're that unhappy, *do* something about it."

I felt my heart start to do this little dance. "You mean, I can drop out and come home?"

"No. I mean . . . look, you used to be all involved in school. Back at Bulging Elk," Grant said. "So do something like that. Cornwall Falls must have dozens of groups, right?"

"No," I said. "It doesn't have anything." Yeah, okay, so I sounded like a 5-year-old.

"Yes, it does," Grant said with a laugh. "You just *said* that you wanted to join a group. I want you to promise me that you'll check out a bunch of them." He said I can't keep not getting settled into the place; if I'm going to be here 4 years, I should work on changing the things that aren't working for me.

"Okay, so transfer, because what isn't working is you being there and me being here," I said. Then I told him all the things I really miss about him, and I was really getting kind of mushy about it, about how much I love being with him—

And then all of a sudden I realized Dean Sobransky was standing right next to me. Listening to the whole thing.

I was *so* busted.

I got off the phone really quickly by saying something loud about how it was always nice to catch up with old classmates. Then I turned to Dean S. with a hopeful smile.

"Well, er, and how is it going, Courtney?" he asked. "Making contact with some alumni you know?"

"Yes," I said. But not as much contact as I'd like.

He said he often dropped by to check on us, since his office was just upstairs (we work in a large basement room). He said he'd like to sit in on my next call, see if he could offer some helpful tips since I'm new at this. Nightmare!

I changed the subject and told him I wanted to get involved in some campus groups and could he tell me about some? He asked me what my interests were. The whole time I talked, he kept opening the file cabinet beside my desk, then closing it. Very weird guy. Has to have something near him in perpetual motion.

"We have the nature club, of course," he said. "And there's the faculty-student birding society."

"Well, I'm not necessarily interested in just watching nature. I'm more interested in *saving* it," I said. "Is there anything about, um, I don't know. Saving the cows?"

"Why do the cows need to be saved? Or, wait—do you mean in a religious sense?"

The guy in my neighboring cubicle wheeled over. "I've got a suggestion." His voice sounded familiar, but I couldn't place it at first. Probably I'd overheard him begging for donations, and since he actually got quite a few, maybe he talked more than most.

"Wittenauer. My favorite fund-raiser! What do you know?" Dean S. asked.

Wittenauer is the guy who pulls in huge donations seemingly without trying. He started talking about a group he's in to protest this hormone that is used campuswide. Dean S. looked very embarrassed, then Wittenauer explained it wasn't a male or female or sex hormone. It's something in the milk that's served in the cafeteria, student center, etc. He explained that he was talking about RBGH.

I couldn't believe it. "You mean the date rape drug? They put that in the *milk* here? What sort of place is this, what sort of society—" I was sputtering irately when Wittenauer put his hand on my arm and told me I was confusing RBGH with GHB.

71

"No, no. Courtney, is it?" He smiled. "No, they don't put that in the milk." Like that wasn't a mistake anyone could make!

"RBGH isn't as bad as GHB," he said. "I mean, we're not talking about men drugging drinks with sedatives to get women to sleep with them."

Dean Sobransky was so embarrassed he could barely talk. "I'm sure nothing like that goes on here," he said. "I, have to . . . have to . . . have to check my messages." He bolted from the room.

Wittenauer went on to explain that RBGH was something like Repulsive Bovine Growth Hormone. It makes cows produce more milk, which is definitely not a good idea. Anyway, isn't milk gross enough on its own, without additives? But then additives are in everything, so why am I surprised? "That sounds disgusting," I said.

"You should come to the next meeting," he said. "It's the RBGH Action Group. We meet on Sunday nights. We're always looking for more members."

Yes! I have found my first group.

Mom called tonight so we could start planning
Thanksgiving. Big surprise. She has planned Thanksgiving in early September for as long as I can remember.
I told her I couldn't be in charge of anything this year
because it's going to be hard enough for me to just
get there. I played the travel hardship card. So ha! Bryan
can bake "all the breads" this year. Which means we'll
see many canned Pillsbury products. Then I asked if she
could bring Grant with her, and she said of course.

So after I talked to her, I called Grant. He was home
but said he couldn't talk long because the guys were waiting for him to go out. I could hear them talking loudly
and laughing in the background. Grant kept asking what
my weekend plans are. He has a bunch. I don't.

"I'm like . . . a loser all of a sudden, Grant," I said.

"Come on, Court. You can definitely find parties to
go to," Grant said, laughing. "You and Oregano—"

"Hey, *don't* make fun of her. She's my best friend
here!" I said.

"So you and Thyme should pick some parties to go to.
Okay?" Grant said. "Read your student newspaper. Read
every flyer you see. Listen to your campus radio station."

He sounded like a public-service announcement. He
sounded so *smug*, him with his roomful of friends, me
with my roomful of . . . knickknacks.

In a way, I'm getting kind of sick of these pep talks.
Like Grant knows how to adjust to a new environment

and I *don't*, or something. Like I'm not evolving. I know more about adjusting than he does. It's really very insulting. Did *he* go 1,000 miles from home? I don't think so.

I'll go out and party all weekend. Then I'll go to that milk meeting. I'll show him that I can adapt as well as anyone.

Mary Jo asked if I wanted to go shopping this afternoon. Which was *really* nice of her. She has this old yellow beater pickup truck that her parents are lending her so she can get settled, but she has to return it to them tonight when she goes home for a weekend visit. (Yay! Weekend of solitude in the room! But I won't really be alone. *Baloney*. Because I'll have Mary Jo's baloney in the fridge to keep me company. Hope it doesn't spoil over the weekend.)

So anyway, she invited me to come along to this place called Farm Supply to stock up on stuff like shampoo and crackers. Even though I didn't need anything for my farm, I thought I should make the effort to be friends. Thinking that she doesn't like me is really upsetting. Ever since the housing-switch fiasco, we've been avoiding each other, except for 9–10 each night, when we both end up here.

So back to the excursion. (Mary Jo is a very good driver. Said she learned how when she was 10, driving around the farm.) The store was like a giant department store with tons of hardware instead of underwear. This is shopping? I thought, as I wandered past aisles of wrenches and drills and chainsaws. Many industrial cleaning products. Snow throwers. Appliances. Candy. There were some semi-interesting canvas overalls and flannel-lined jeans. That and a ton of bright orange and camouflage clothing under the HUNTER'S PARADISE sign.

Mary Jo really knew her way around the place. I stayed with her because I was afraid of getting lost. She has some very helpful skills, it turns out. Like figuring out what size picture hangers we need for our room.

"How far would we have to drive to reach an actual mall?" I asked as we stood in line. There was a special on Twizzlers so I bought 8 or 9 family-size packages, since I didn't want to leave empty-handed. They looked sort of massive as I watched them go down the conveyor belt. But, oh well, Super Size Me.

"Hm. To reach any mall?" she asked. "Or a good mall?"

"Good," I said. "As in not the lame outlets on the edge of town."

"Well, probably about two hours," Mary Jo said, putting all her horse hairstyling and skin care products on the belt. "Why?"

WHY? Wasn't it obvious?

E-mailed Grant after Mary Jo left for the weekend and told him that Mary Jo is a bit weird but basically nice. He e-mailed back that she seemed nice whenever he talked to her and that I was lucky to have a good roommate. I guess he's right. Especially if she goes home on random weekends.

FRIDAY NIGHT . . .

Do they have to put bar code stickers on pens like this? You can't pull them off or it leaves a sticky film. But then you have to stare at the bar code as you write. Not very inspiring. Yes, I am just 1 of a billion humans writing in a journal today. Not even the best journal or best writer. A speck, a UPC code.

Sorry. Tonight wasn't *that* bad, really. And I do have the room to myself, so maybe I should be doing something more fun than writing in here about the sorry decline of fountain pens and the increasing depersonalization of our society. (Yes, I've been reading too much poli sci.)

Thyme and I hung out at the student center listening to bad student jazz in the bad student coffeehouse, a section in the center that they've roped off and tried to make hip. But it has bad coffee, all of which tastes like hazelnut whether you order hazelnut or not, and bright lighting. I guess it might work in the morning if you were trying to wake up. And liked hazelnut. Maybe.

But our pain and suffering was all worth it, because we met some girls who told us about a party tomorrow night. It's at a big house off campus that is known for having great parties. These girls said it's like considered a failure if the police don't show up. What? They have parties like that here?

SATURDAY NIGHT . . . DATE? NO THANK YOU.
I MEAN I DON'T KNOW.

Got home about 10 hours ago. 10 minutes I mean. Whatever. Can't think straight can't walk straight.

Party was sooooo fun. Talked with a billion people. Danced. Ate hummus. Yes!

Some guys wanted to dance with me but I said no. No because I love Grant. The guys from pool table also there. Kept slamming into us and spilling beer on me. Suede coat is ruined but oh well.

Okay so Thyme is dragging her sleeping bag into the room because MJ "Don't Call Me MJ!" is away for weekend. While she is gone I called Grant and this is what I said on his machine I think:

"If you were a pen I'd be the bar code sticker."

Couldn't stop laughing when I hung up. I hope he gets home before his roomie.

Wait. Why is he not home? It's middle of the night.

Oops. Different time zone. I'm waiting an hour then calling him. He has a right to be out as late as me.

1:10 A.M. Sleepy.

1:30 A.M. Thyme is putting horse hair products on her face. "Be careful, or you'll grow a tail," I said and we are laughing so loud that Krystyne told us to be quiet. Rules against laughing at this dumb place.

2:10 A.M. Called him again. Told him to call me no matter when he gets in.

So far I have spent the morning doing 5 things:

1. Trying not to puke.
2. Remembering embarrassing things I did and said last night and cringing and then wanting to puke.
3. Waiting for Grant to call.
4. Waiting for ibuprofen to work so this god-awful headache goes away. (Am writing this with one eye closed. Ow.)
5. Waiting for Thyme to stop telling me what's wrong with patriarchal society.

"Hey, I wasn't even *raised* by my dad, so why are you lecturing me?" I said, wanting to annoy her so much that she'd just realize I was in pain and didn't want to chat. Especially not, with feeling so embarrassed over being blown off by my boyfriend and dancing with people I don't know and discussing the meaning of life and the relation of animals to God in between shouting out song lyrics. But I guess that was sort of sucking up to the patriarchal society in her eyes to even care about a boy (like she doesn't have a crush on Ben, she only comes in every day to see me at work so she can see him, and she wanted to dance with him last night when he showed up, but he didn't want to dance, he only wanted to talk to me about the concept of alienation not being so alienating when you've had a few beers).

"Courtney, it goes much, much deeper than you realize," she said.

"I know," I said. "I was just joking."

"Well, it's not something to joke about. Remember, no one is truly free when others are oppressed."

She says that about every situation that bothers her. Which is every situation.

Now she's examining everything on my dresser for environmental correctness. Maybe having Thyme for a roommate would not be such a good idea.

"You know, the binge drinking that goes on in today's college society is just awful," she said. "We never would have gotten so plowed last night if those guys hadn't kept filling our glasses with beer. That was so *patronizing* of them, to just assume we wanted more, like *we* didn't know how much we wanted."

"Maybe if we hadn't kept drinking it," I said. "They wouldn't have refilled . . . um . . . " Really vivid memories of keg beer were flooding my stomach. If a stomach has memories. Which I think it does.

LATER THAT SAME DAY. MUCH TOO MUCH LATER, IN MY OPINION . . .

Grant finally called. Let's just say that it did not go well. I needed him to tell me he was home visiting his parents and grandmother in Denver and that's why he wasn't home at 1 and 2 A.M. That's what I thought he was going to say. The only explanation. But that wasn't it.

He was at a party. He had fun. He went out to breakfast at 2 A.M. He wouldn't stop talking about how much *fun* it was.

"So how was your night?" he asked after he'd finished telling me the details of his late-night donut selection. "You sounded kind of wild. What did you mean about the pen thing?"

I didn't know what he was talking about. "You must be talking about someone else's message," I said, sounding hopelessly and pathetically jealous. "I wasn't wild and I never mentioned a pen." Although as soon as I said that, I remembered.

"Whatever you say, Court." Then I heard him yawning. It made me miss him so much that I burst out crying. Why couldn't I be there to lie around on a Sunday with him?

Ended up with him spending 10 minutes trying to cheer me up. The whole time I could hear a football game playing in the background. How could he listen to Broncos and console me from darkest depths of depression at the same time? How rude.

Major mistake tonight. Very embarrassing. Did I leave my brain in Colorado?

I thought I was at the anti-growth-hormones-in-milk meeting. Didn't see Wittenauer (what is his first name?), but decided he must be running late. Meeting started. A lot of people had been there before, but a lot hadn't, according to the group leader. So we went around the circle and everyone was supposed to say something about themselves. Knew something was odd when the 6 people before me all stated their sexual preferences. Didn't understand how that related to dairy products. I didn't want to state mine because it seemed like I might be the only hetero there, but I did say, "Hi, I'm Courtney, and I think I'm at the wrong meeting."

"It's okay, Courtney," the group leader said. "Everyone feels shy at first. It's normal to be uncomfortable, but no one's going to judge you here."

The woman sitting next to me reached over and put her hand on my knee. "We're all friends, and nothing you say will go beyond this room."

"Okay, but um . . . is this about milk?"

16 blank faces stared at me.

"I'm supposed to be at a meeting protesting hormonal supplements," I said.

The group leader, Jay, cleared his throat. "This is the meeting for Bisexual and Gay Republican Hearts. We try to introduce students who have something in common?"

Agh! I was at dating club for non-hetero non-Democrats! Stupid me got initials confused.

"You're not here to infiltrate our group, are you?" one paranoid guy asked.

"You're not here to find out our names?" someone else asked.

"You're not free on Saturday night, are you?" the girl next to me asked.

"My sister's a lesbian," I said. "But um . . . I don't know if she votes Republican or Democrat. Excuse me."

How embarrassing!

Sunday nights. Not *Monday* nights.

When I told Thyme about it, she said, "Well, of course. I could have told you that." Then she rattled off every campus group's meeting time, place, agenda. So why *didn't* she tell me that when I mentioned I was dashing off to the meeting? Does she *want* me to fail? Does she *want* hormones in milk?

If I had a photographic memory, I wouldn't go through life constantly embarrassing myself. I would also be nicer to my friends.

Sitting at BF on my break. It's raining. I should be studying, but, oh well. Ben is studying and isn't that enough for
both of us? I should also be writing Grant a letter (we
decided not to call this week in order to save $$). But I'm
not in the mood. Can't tell him how I blew first attempt
to get involved in community.

Mark seems to be walking a tightrope. Business is
slow but instead of cleaning and refilling bins, he is
touching up his nails by the register.

"I don't know. I don't like the double coat so much."
He just held out his hand, admiring the nail polish.
Jennifer went by, saw him, and told him to check the
bagels baking in the back, and not to get any Revlon on
them.

Prediction: Mark will be getting a burned bagel
sticker next to his name on the schedule.

Systems of pluses and minuses she uses is really asi-
nine. Good service = cute little muffin sticker and nick-
name "muffin" all week. Mark would probably like that.

LATER. DUDE ...

Work deteriorated majorly after I wrote the above.

Hate this job. Hate how it makes me spell everything
wrong.

"Jennifer?" I asked as I anti-bacterialized the slicer.
"Why does bagel have to be spelled wrong in the store
names? I mean, it would rhyme even if we spelled it right.

It's a homonym. You know, like um . . . time? And thyme, the herb?"

She patted me on the shoulder. "I think we know what we're doing, McCartney."

I had a *name tag* on. "It's Courtney," I said.

"Oh my gosh, what was I thinking?" Jennifer laughed. "You remind me of this girl who used to work here, last year. *Sorry*," she said in this incredibly phony voice.

Later on, Ben told me that McCartney was a really good friend of his. But she hated working at BF and she hated CF and she and Jennifer got into a huge fight. She quit and after freshman year she transferred to another school.

"So do I remind you of McCartney? And were her parents Beatles freaks? I mean, did she have a brother named Lennon or Ringo?" I asked.

Ben laughed. "Harrison and Lennon, I think. Twins. You do remind me of her a little. But I think when Jennifer says it, it's not a compliment, so look out."

Does this mean I get to quit and transfer, too?

Oh joy oh joy oh joy. When?

Got home from phoning unsuspecting alumni and received very disturbing e-mails from naïve Mom. She has suddenly gone from not dating to being romanced by a chat-room guy.

She forwarded me a couple of e-mails he wrote and asked my opinion. Didn't he seem like a great guy to me? she asked. SEEM being the operative word here. Here's our e-mail exchange:

> Mom—
> I'm slightly worried about this Internet
> Romance Idea of yours. What about meeting
> guys in person? What about that guy in your
> book club? You said he was nice and sweet and
> you liked the same books. You really need to
> be careful. Haven't you told me a hundred
> billion times not to do risky things like this?
> Promise me you won't agree to meet this guy
> in person!!! —C

> Bryan—
> You have got to keep an eye on Mom! She's
> getting swept away by guy in chat room who is
> at best a psycho and at worst a serial killer.
> Don't let her make any dates, and keep track of
> her, wherever she goes. —C

Courtney—
She's already met the chat-room guy. He's fine,
harmless, bald, boring as hell. Don't worry.
—Bryan

Like I trust Bryan's opinion on anything involving
romance, the heart, etc.? He pined after Beth for 5 years
and then somehow convinced her to date him. Still don't
understand that, 1 year later.

Anyway, I should be glad Mom is at least showing
interest in the dating thing. If she finds someone she
really likes, that will be great. I just don't want him to be
the kind of person who turns out to be—well, just like
Dad.

Must call Alison now and ask her to intervene. Mom
will listen to Alison because she's the oldest and because
she's—well—better at this stuff than me. Has had stable
relationship with Jessie for almost a year. Of course, they
go to the same *college*, so that helps.

I really do need to stop resenting everyone else on the
planet. Especially when they're my siblings.

You know how sometimes your friends don't get along? And you're the link and you feel really awkward because of it? Tried to hang out with Mark and Thyme today. I had already planned on lunch with Thyme, and Mark invited himself along. Mark had already told me he thought Thyme's hair was cool but that he hated the rest of her neo-hippie look. Since he comments on everyone's hair and clothes, I didn't think much of it—until they got into a raging argument while we waited for a table. Thyme insisted we wait so we could sit in non-smoking; Mark insisted we sit at the counter so he could smoke. Since I'm used to hanging out with Beth, who used to smoke, it didn't really matter one way or the other to me. Thyme thought I was taking Mark's side and stormed out. I thought maybe I should go after her but just then one of the waitresses walked by with a yummy-looking giant salad on her tray and I decided not to.

"You're not having a malt?" Mark asked after we ordered. "Are you high?"

(Why does everyone keep asking me that?)

I laughed. "No, actually, I'm LI."

"You're from Long Island? I thought you were from Denver."

I hit his arm. "No, it's my stomach. It's a condition."

Mark unwrapped his straw as he thought this over. Then his nose wrinkled, like he'd just thought something sort of gross. "You have a problem with your large intestine?"

I couldn't stop laughing. "No! Well, sort of. I'm lactose intolerant."

"Oh. What a drag. That's kind of like me and cheap hair products." He shivered. "I break out in hives if it's not salon quality."

Mark slurped his chocolate malt when it came, topped with this perfect pinnacle of whipped cream. My mouth watered. Of course it was impossible for me to tell him that I really wanted a sip now. Have to wait until we're better friends.

Thyme came in to visit me at work today—she said it was
to make up for being so crabby yesterday, and because
she always needs to drink extra coffee when it's raining
steadily, but I think it's only because she's obsessed with
Ben. He's a great guy and she's my best friend here, so I'll
do what I can, but I think she pretty much blew it today.

She came in and tried to start this in-depth conversation with Ben, telling him her opinions on men, women,
world peace, harmony, life after death, etc.

I mean, all she really had to do was ask him questions
about himself or tell him the onion bagels were good, or
something simple like that. But no. She got into the con-
cepts of how you need to open yourself up and be Zenlike
and how the Bagle Finagle stores could really use some
feng shui.

"So where are you from? California?" Ben asked her.

"Um, no, outside Chicago," Thyme said.

"Really? Where? I grew up in Chicago," Ben said.

"Oh, um." Thyme looked sort of uncomfortable all of
a sudden. "Are those tomatoes organic?"

I put my hands on my hips. "What do *you* think?"

"Is that margarine or unsalted butter?" she asked
next.

Ben gave me this sideways glance, like: what's up
with that? "So where did you say you were from?" he
asked.

"Well, technically I was born a little north of Chicago.

On the lake," Thyme said.

"Uh huh. Where exactly?" Ben asked.

"Ummmmm . . . in Sheboygan," Thyme finally said.

"But that's in Wisconsin," Ben said. "You said you were from Chicago. It's not really all that close."

"Okay, well maybe technically I guess you could say I lived there my whole life. But inside, I always considered myself a *Chicagoan*," Thyme said, sounding really lame to me all of a sudden. Who lies about where they're from? What's the point?

Just then Jennifer came up and told us our break was over, and had been over for 5 minutes, didn't we pay attention to the clock? It was like getting caught talking in class. But to be honest, I was sort of relieved.

"The phony Buddhist from Sheboygan. Now I've seen everything," Ben muttered as we slid sheets of hot bagels into baskets. "How do you know her exactly?"

"Oh, um, she lives across the hall from me," I said. Not getting into the fact that she was the closest thing to a friend I had on campus. If she's a phony, I guess it's better to know now. But I thought she had passionate ideas about fibers and fabrics and free-range animals. I don't think she has a chance in hell with Ben. I wonder if she knows that now.

What a weird, great day. Still trying to absorb everything that happened. Like soggy ground, I can only absorb so much more at this point.

Last night's rah-rah bonfire was rained out, literally—the rain put out the fire. Does not smell like team spirit. Smells like mildew. Even outside. Today was still drizzling and soggy; everyone showing off latest umbrella styles and rain gear at the football game.

When we got there, it turned out that it was "Highlighting Student Activities Day." And all these different groups, from dancers to backgammon clubs, etc., had booths set up with paper banners that had been highlighted with neon green, pink, orange, etc. Very colorful, except the rain had gotten the banners wet and the letters were all runny and streaked and it was hard to determine what each group was, unless you stopped, made eye contact, collected handout.

We circulated: me, Thyme, Mary Jo, Tricia, Annemarie, Peña. Everyone. It was funny because we were all moving at different speeds; some of us raced by certain booths, while others stopped to sign up. And vice versa. I was thinking maybe this place wasn't so bad. There really is something for everyone here. It truly is a microcosm or macrocosm or, at the very least, cosmic. In the background, football was going on. Mud flying through the air. Random cheers and sounds of helmets crushing into pads.

We were standing by this booth that was the only one smart enough to have a banner not written in high-lighter—they had a real sewn banner made of cloth, as if the group has been here forever. Students for Change. And they had signs up that said QUESTION AUTHORITY and EDUCATE YOURSELF and HOW LIBERAL IS YOUR LIBERAL ARTS INSTITUTION?

"Have you heard about the Campus Badicals?" this really nice girl asked me. She handed me a brochure.

"These people are like, so on the fringe?" Tricia said when the girl started talking to someone else. "Everything's going really well here, everything's *fine*? But they have to change everything or complain about it or whatever?"

"I don't know—there's always room for improvement," Annemarie said. "Don't you think, Courtney?"

"Definitely," I said. "Like, *lots* of room." Everyone sort of moved ahead, but I was still checking out the stuff on the table.

Just then the cheerleaders started up with their "C—F—C! C—F—C!" chant. I joked to the girl behind the table how it was really distressing to hear that our college initials represented a harmful chemical. And that we were all supposed to chant along, like we were cheering for the destruction of the ozone layer, like CFCs hadn't been phased out, or as if they should be phased back *in* or something.

Suddenly everyone at the booth was gazing at me like I had just invented tofu.

"Finally. A fresh voice," the girl said.

Like I was the new Dalai Lama. A freshperson born in the wilderness, the 7th child of . . . well, whatever. They all jumped up and introduced themselves and shook my hand and insisted I come to a meeting tomorrow.

"Cool," Annemarie said. "Maybe I'll go with you."

"I don't even know what you were talking about." Mary Jo was looking at me with some sort of newfound respect, or maybe just bafflement. Impressed that I could impress someone, I guess.

"So what do they want you to, like, *do*?" Tricia asked. "I don't know what you guys were talking about. But that group is always in the campus newspaper?"

Thyme was suddenly nowhere to be found. Odd, because this was totally her kind of group, too. I'll ask her to go with me and Annemarie tomorrow.

Tonight we all rented multiple movies, and I must go because next showing is starting.

Went to the Campus Badicals meeting today. Annemarie went with me, also Thyme. We were kind of intimidated, so it was good to go as a group. We had tried to check out the group's history beforehand, but Krystyne didn't know much except that they got arrested once. Thyme said she wouldn't mind getting arrested; the weekends had been sort of boring lately, right? We laughed nervously as we entered the basement of the student union.

Room was half full. It turned out my idea to revise the college initials was the topic of the meeting. Someone mentioned that I had a brilliant insight and could I share it? So I did, and all of sudden it was the main and only issue of the group. Someone insisted a focus/splinter group be formed immediately, then everyone joined the focus group.

It was so exciting I completely forgot about the RBGH meeting afterward, came running home to call Grant. But then remembered our pledge not to call this week. Then called anyway. He wasn't home, so I hung up quickly so as not to be busted on breaking the not-calling pledge.

I want to tell him everything. It feels very weird to go through a weekend without him. How can I be going through the most exciting stuff yet and not call him? Okay, so I've been e-mailing 3, 4 times a day. Maybe that's enough, but it's still not the same.

Came home after work and Mary Jo was on the phone. Which was lousy because I really wanted to call Grant. Our 1-week break was over and I was dying to talk to him. I sat on the edge of the bed and waited. She was laughing and talking about cows and then about how helpful a good dog can be on the farm, and how much she missed her dogs, and what the best kind of dogs are, etc.

So then Mary Jo says, "Well, it's been fun talking to you, but Courtney just got home, so . . . " I expected her to say, "'Bye, Mom," or "'Bye, Aunt Peggy" or whatever. Then she said, "So here she is, Grant. Good luck in biology!" She handed the phone to me as I nearly fell off the bed. Grant and Mary Jo are hitting it off, sounding like old buds? They're having better phone conversations than we do, and we haven't even *talked* for a week, and now somehow Mary Jo has an in with him and I don't?

How can I be jealous of Mary Jo? But I am. She and Grant have so much in common. She probably knows tons about being a vet; has probably delivered baby cows before, the way they do on those prairie kids TV shows. She can talk to the animals. So can Grant.

I felt really sick to my stomach all of a sudden. There was so much I hadn't considered yet, so much to get really worried about. If there's a girl like this here, there's definitely a girl like that there. In Grant's classes. Horse-whispering girl from Colorado ranch. Rodeo-riding gal from Wyoming. Someone he'd been talking to all week when he *hadn't* been talking to me. Okay, so it was my idea to not call, to save money, but he didn't have to just go along with it, without a fight.

"Courtney? Are you there?" Grant asked when I didn't say anything, because jealousy had commandeered my brain.

"Um, I don't feel very good. I'll call you back," I told him. I hung up the phone.

Mary Jo gave me this little innocent smile. "You're not feeling well? Is there anything I can get you?"

Fantasy reply: "How about a new roommate who isn't cute and knows nothing about vet science. That would be good."

Actual reply: "No, I'll be okay, but thanks." Returned little innocent smile. Ran to the bathroom, splashed cold water on my face. Tried to stop freaking out.

Will call Grant tomorrow morning when she's not here.

Working for Jennifer is killing me. Today she started this new stupid system where there's a board with our names on it, and we have to mark down where we are "at any given time." Like, even when we go to the bathroom. She has this board and when you leave your "post" you have to put a "code" on it, and a "time estimate." Like I'm telling people what I'm in the bathroom for? Is she insane?

"She needs more codes," Mark said after she explained the board to us and went back to her office. "What do I write down when I'm going to the bathroom to sneak a smoke?"

"And what do I write for 'went to bathroom to escape the sound of her *voice*?'" Ben asked.

"What is the code for 'I quit'?" I asked.

It's a good thing everyone I work with is so cool. Because it takes a village to counterbalance Jennifer's uncool.

Someone was trying to put up a flyer for a local band's concert, and then someone came by to post a sign for a meeting of Kids with Kids, a group that helps people like my stepsister. Jennifer came along and took them all off the bulletin board as soon as they had left.

"If you were going to do that, you should have told them," I said. "They could post them somewhere else and save paper."

"Not to mention the fact that there's such a thing as free speech," Ben said.

"And there's also such a thing as turning a profit," Jennifer said. "We can't afford to post all these flyers when we have wealthy advertisers who pay us to put up things." She flounced around, picking up stray crumbs and straw wrappers.

"Yeah, and this campus needs more ad space for magazine subscription services," I told Ben as I scrubbed the cutting boards. "Because we all need to get *Ice Fishing* and *Wisconsin Brat Hunter*."

Ben started laughing. "You don't *hunt* brats, Courtney."

"Oh. Do they just come to you, then?" I asked.

Jennifer slammed down an empty napkin dispenser in front of me and nearly broke the glass counter. "There's nothing wrong with sausage. If you'd just try some, you'd know. Okay?"

"I know," I said. "I've had hot dogs."

"It's not the same at all," Jennifer scoffed.

Mark put his hand on my shoulder. "Don't get too mad at Courtney. She's led a sheltered life, you know. She's a brat virgin."

Brat Virgin. I love it. It's like the name of a band.

Mark, Ben, and I were laughing so hard we couldn't hear what Jennifer said. It was something like "You guys get back to work" blah blah blah. The usual. We ignored her.

Thyme sat down next to me on the quad today. Her tirade went something like this:

"I'm transferring. This place is a joke! Do you know there's only one women's studies course available next semester for freshpeople? I can't believe I didn't look into this before I got here. I just *assumed*. They told me the department needs more professors but there's a hiring freeze. So then I tried to find my adviser, but he changed his office hours, so I sat outside in the hall waiting for like an hour before someone bothered to tell me he wasn't coming in. They just want their paycheck and that's it. And the way they turned your work-study job from a law apprenticeship into groveling for money? It's unforgivable."

Why does she have to be so negative all the time? Why does she say out loud the things I'm thinking and trying to avoid?

"Thanks a lot," I told Thyme. "You really depressed the hell out of me." I got up and started to walk away.

She ran after me and apologized, then dragged me into the student center and insisted on buying me a smoothie. It was too runny and not cold enough and made with Kool-Aid and canned-tasting fruit instead of fresh frozen, but I didn't bother going into it. What's that saying about learning to accept the things you can't change? One of those 12 steps Beth hopped through on her way to becoming unaddicted to cigarettes. So I'll never have a good smoothie again. So . . . that's okay. I guess.

Then I thought, maybe it *isn't* okay. Maybe it *can* be changed. Screw acceptance. I'd get a business loan, open my own health food store, since there are a grand total of zero here. Or wait—Gerry, my old boss, was always talking about expanding. Gerry loved me. He could open a Truth or Dairy here, in Wauzataukie. I could manage it!

I called him as soon as I got back tonight from groveling for money. Now I'm groveling for a job. He wasn't in, but I left a message. It's just so obvious I don't belong at BF. I belong at a place like T or D.

Talked to Gerry today. It was so good to hear his voice. And that really almost freaks me out.

"Courtney! My favorite former employee!" he said when he answered the phone. Well, after he got past his trademark "Truth or Dairy, this is Gerry!" He gets so excited about it, like he's the first person who's ever rhymed before. Like he hasn't made the *same* rhyme year after year, day after day.

I told him how much I missed working with him and how working for BF was awful and then I begged him to think about opening a new store here. "There's nothing in town anything like T or D, you'd make so much money, and—"

"I don't know, Courtney." He was completely dragging his Birkenstocked feet.

"Come on, Gerry. We'll call it Truth or Dairyland! Or American Truth, or America's Dairyland!" I said. Total on-the-spot-new-state brainstorm.

Gerry wasn't impressed. He told me that sounded like a course title I must be taking. "Sorry, Courtney. But I really don't have the capital to expand right now. And even if I did . . . as much as I respect and trust you, Courtney, uh, Wauzataukie, Wisconsin, would not be my first choice." He made it sound like this town is a bad place or something just because of its tongue-twister name. "There are still Colorado cities I want to conquer. Wait, conquer isn't the right word, it's too violent. I'd never go in with the idea of starting anything. I don't want a smoothie war on my hands." He started laughing. "That would be quite a sticky mess!"

"My *life* is a sticky mess!" I interrupted him. "I'm working for a corporate giant that chews up local competition and spits it out. They're like the Microsoft of bagel makers!"

"Oh. How unfortunate."

I started crying. In front of *Gerry*. (Okay, not in front technically, but close enough to be humiliating.) I told him all the problems I'd been having with the manager and how she kept comparing me to this "problem employee."

"Don't put up with that—quit!" Gerry said. "Isn't that what you usually do when you're trying to prove a point?" He reminded me of how I'd quit twice last fall when I was going through what he calls my "unstable senior-year period." (Once a guidance counselor, always insane.)

"I can't quit," I said, ignoring the way he was typecasting me as a quitter. "There aren't any other jobs here. That's why I'm asking you to create one."

"Sorry. I just can't," he said. He sounded really sincere about it. "I need to keep the business close to home."

Home. Yeah, I've heard of that place.

Then the conversation took a really weird turn.

"While I have you on the phone, Courtney, have you heard what happened to Beth?"

"No," I said slowly. I hadn't talked to her or gotten an

e-mail in the last week. "Why?"

"Well, she and your brother . . . they apparently got into a fight yesterday," Gerry said. "And Beth went out and bought some cigarettes on her way into work. And she was lighting one while she was driving, and I think a cell phone was involved, and, well—she crashed her car into the sign here."

The Shops at Canyon Boulevard sign? I couldn't believe it. Why hadn't she told me? Called me in a panic? "Was she hurt?" I asked.

"No, not at all. But her parents are positively livid," Gerry said. "And the strip mall advisory board is none too happy with her. Business is down since yesterday. They want her banned from parking in our lot."

"That's ridiculous! Everyone has accidents," I said.

"Yes. But not everyone jumps out of their car and starts yelling at the sign in front of valuable patrons," Gerry said.

Beth sounds really stressed out. I have *got* to get in touch with her. Maybe she will transfer here after all.

Talked to Beth. She told me what happened and we laughed for a really long time. She said she went on a rant because she was mad at having to make that turn in all the traffic and the person behind her honked at her, etc. I could just picture it all *so clearly*. I probably would have been in the car with her, but then, if I had, she wouldn't have been smoking or talking on the phone, so maybe not. Anyway, she's fine, except that Gerry is asking her to go door-to-door and apologize to all the other businesses in the strip mall for her behavior.

She threw out the cigarettes as soon as it happened, and then called Bryan and they made up and life is hunky-dory and non-smoking again. She said she tried to call me but didn't get me, so she called Grant instead, and he calmed her down. Superior boyfriend even helps my friends.

Thyme and I went to the campus co-op house tonight for dinner. They were having an open house to recruit new members. We had to pay, but assumed we'd get awesome organic food. Probably our expectations were unreasonable. We're never going back.

Most disgusting meal ever. Mishmash of mush and tofu. Flavorless. Shapeless. Looked like prison food. Inedible.

Then afterward they said they had room for only *one* new member, so all the people there who were interested needed to write an essay with an application fee and then have an interview and then cook for all the existing members, just to get in so they could eat more crappy meals.

Thyme and I left before dessert. We were laughing so hard and still so hungry that she took me out for dinner at Koffee Kitchen. Drank too much coffee and now can't sleep.

Wonder what Grant is doing tonight. Probably has more fun things to do on Friday nights. Probably out.

Just called him, and his roommate said he hadn't seen him since 2.

Since 2? But it's 11 there. Doesn't he at least need to come home and, I don't know, *call me*?

Work this morning was very strange. Jennifer kept talking about an exciting new menu addition, but wouldn't say what it actually was. She said we all needed to be "on board" for the "Bagle Brainstorm" that was coming our way on Monday.

Mark rolled his eyes. "We're so thrilled. What now? Blue cheese bagels?" I looked at his name tag. He had recently punched out a new one on the label maker, so it now said Marc.

"How about blue cheese and blueberry?" Ben asked.

"Or could we get goat cheese involved somehow?" I asked.

Jennifer shook her head. "You guys are *so* weird. Just be ready, that's all I'm saying. And what's with that?" She pointed to Mark/Marc's new name tag.

"It's called a name change," Marc said. "I'm exploring my identity. Do you *mind*?"

"No, but don't do it on company time," Jennifer said.

After work, I met Thyme back at the dorm. Mary Jo was hanging out with Kirsten in their room, so Thyme and I stayed in my room. Very awkward. The 4 of us kept running back and forth to get stuff we all wanted. Reminded me of a fight I got into at a sleepover at Beth's house in junior high. We divided into 2 parties, except I left my sleeping bag, backpack, etc., in the wrong room. Ended up having to apologize just to get my pajamas. Why didn't I just go home? Not sure.

Shocking development at Badicals meeting today! We were all supposed to discuss ways to fight the college initials, or at least the chanting of them at football games. I didn't really have any big ideas, but since the major concept was mine, I didn't feel too much pressure. Thyme was going to do a presentation on how the school could easily become known as Feminist Falls or something like that (sounds like a product advertised by mothers and daughters); she was trying to come up with alternative names but had some really bad ones like that.

Anyway, we trekked into the meeting and this guy was already talking, doing his presentation. It was Wittenauer, the milk-hormone protester and champion fund-raiser! He's trying to undermine, change, revolutionize the place while simultaneously getting people to send in huge checks.

Wittenauer agrees with my idea to change the school name. He's also protesting the mascot, for promoting cruelty to corn and veggies in general. He said that to use their image to promote the college is just wrong.

"Okay, but not as bad as using an animal," I said. "Like the CU Buffaloes, when they run Ralphie out onto the field, or Cam the Ram at CSU—"

Everyone jumped all over me! They had like a dozen prepared arguments to shoot me down with. "It's *exactly* as bad!" Wittenauer started describing all the things that are done to harm defenseless crops—and defenseless mascots. I was wondering how he knew so much about it, and asked if he was an Ag major.

"No," he said, and his face got all red. "I'm Corny."

Agh! Top school fund-raiser is top Badical and also school mascot.

Corny believes in change from within. Which is why he's the mascot while simultaneously protesting the idea of the mascot. But no one can know Wittenauer is the mascot because "the position is secret and it's a Cornwall Falls tradition and only the people in this room know it's me," he insisted. "I only reveal my identity here because I think I can help our cause while remaining anonymous. The mascot gets chosen by the previous mascot by getting tapped on the shoulder. Nothing is ever spoken."

Wait a second, I thought. He tapped me on the shoulder at that outdoor party. Did that mean . . . ? But no, he's only a junior. I refuse the position anyway.

Afterward, Thyme and I went downstairs to play pool. Saw those guys who think Thyme's name is hilarious. When they saw us, one of them said, "Hey, look, it's Parsley and Sage!"

Thyme said she's heard this her whole life, and she's learned to just ignore it. But I couldn't ignore it because at first they were actually really funny. They kept calling me Oregano and the Un-named Spice Girl.

But then they totally turned on me and said, "Where did you go to high school again? Rutting Elk?" "No, I think it was Molting Elk," another one said.

"Bugling Elk," I said.

They started to make fun of it even more, and this weird feeling came over me, a feeling I'd only had a few times before, and usually only at assemblies or while signing yearbooks: intense pride in high school. Best place ever. Should never have left it and come to this place where guys roam student union looking for girls to pick on. I was V.P. there. I was *somebody*. I didn't hang around pool tables getting insulted by freshman boys in matching baseball caps.

Just wait until I change the school's name and their dumb caps are like *null and void*.

Why does everything have to happen at once? Just when I thought I was getting settled here, finding friends, feeling at home, blah blah blah, *wham!* How about *this* to ruin your life, Courtney?

Bagle Brainstorm: Bagle Finagle's meat license or whatever they needed finally came through. Now we don't just sell cold-cut sandwiches, which, okay, weren't that great to begin with. But now we're going to sell Bratwurst Bites, Bacon Bacles, Brat-in-a-Blanket, Knockwurst Knots, Sausage Snaps, ugh, all variation on the same theme, weird meats inside bagels.

Hello? Isn't one of the really great qualities about bagels that they *don't* have meat inside them???

And if that wasn't bad enough, Jennifer announced that she was putting me in charge of the "New Product Team."

"But I'm a vegetarian," I said. "Can't I be in charge of chopping the non-meat items? What about salad in a blanket?"

"Where does the dressing go?" Jennifer asked.

"In the blanket," I said.

"No way. Too soggy," she said.

She has an answer for everything.

"Courtney, life is change. You either accept that and move on, or, well, I don't know. Here." She handed me my new apron. Which says in big letters:

KNOCK KNOCK! (*right* across the chest)

WHO'S THERE?
KNOCKWURST KNOTS!

I am supposed to wear this thing? And have people ask about my "knock knock" apron? The humiliation is going to be endless.

Jennifer only put me in charge because she knows I'd hate it and is trying to break my will, like something out of that Paul Newman movie involving a prisoner and eggs and a chain gang, only I'm not in "the hole," I'm in "the hell" of promoting pork-filled dough.

"Courtney, we've got to compete. We need to stay competitive. Brat Wurstenburger really cuts into our lunch business," Jennifer said, "and market studies in other Bagle Finagles show that there's a real need for these lunch items."

"But that place has been here for a hundred years. You're the one who's trying to cut into their business!" Found myself in the incredibly awkward position of standing up for Brat Wurstenburger. Grandpa might be proud, but my self-esteem was crumbling to the ground.

"I'm going to quit," I told Marc when the meeting broke up and we were standing there holding our new *brown* aprons.

"So am I," Marc said. "I refuse to wear this . . . this . . . whatever." His apron said MAKE MY BLT ON A BACLE! in big yellow letters.

"This is just her shameless attempt to like . . . dominate me," I said. "And she wants me to quit. But you know what? I'm not going to give her the satisfaction."

"Yeah. Neither am I," said Marc. And he grabbed the label maker and started making another new name tag for himself. At least I thought it was for him. Then he handed me the label. "Sucker."

Right now Mary Jo has soft music on, some country-western singer singing romantic crap . . . what's up with that? It's either just her bad taste in music, or she's in love.

"Why do you have to be so far away . . . " the song twangs, over and over, which only makes me think of Grant.

Does it make her think of him, too? Caught her yesterday staring closely at one of his photos. She said it was because she thought she saw a horse in the background—which was true, the picture was from when we visited a vet school—and wanted to know what kind it was, but now I'm not sure. Wasn't she really checking out Grant? And what was with those long phone conversations they have when he calls and I'm not home? Can't she just let the machine pick up?

Why did I have to get a roommate who communicates so well with animals and with my boyfriend?

I'm working at Funders right now. Have to write this down because it's very funny.

Corny/Wittenauer just came over and said, "So Courtney, it's all set for Saturday, right? The football game?"

We have big plans for our CFC protest. I'd ironed them out with Corny at the end of our meeting on Sunday and he was calling everyone to coordinate.

Anyway, the ever-present Dean Sobransky was hanging around. He thinks that just because he's our supervisor and we work downstairs from his office he should drop by constantly. He happened to overhear. "What's that?" he asked. "What's all set?"

"Oh, Courtney and I. We're uh, having breakfast," he said.

Dean S. raised his eyebrow. "I didn't mean to pry."

"No, of course you didn't," Wittenauer said, sort of winking at me.

"You're such a genius at this job. If you don't mind giving Courtney some tips. You know," Dean S. said in a tone I guess he thought was low enough for me not to hear. "Show her the way."

"Which way is that?" Wittenauer joked.

Out of town? I'm thinking. Really fast? Dean S. is way too nosey. He should not be in charge of Student Affairs, he should leave that to us. Not that I'm thinking of having one, just, you know. He's overinvolved. Needs his own life.

Nearly fainted from shock when I got home tonight. There was an actual boy in our room. I was wrong! Mary Jo isn't after Grant—she has a boyfriend of her own.

She'd been talking about someone named Joe for a while, but I honestly haven't been around much and I wasn't paying attention. I sort of thought it was one of her brothers.

Instead it's this freshman who is tall and skinny and has lots of nervous tics. But Mary Jo loves him.

Mary Jo and Joe. That's like a double Joe. (In other words, a large coffee?) If they have any kids, they can name him or her Jo-Joe Johannsen. If he lets her keep her name. Which he wouldn't. I can just tell.

But I'm hoping they don't get married, have kids, or even stay together for one more week, because even though Mary Jo and I have nothing in common and I can't wait to switch roommates and live off campus ASAP, I think she deserves way better than this guy. I guess he is her study partner, because they met in chemistry and got to know each other in class and while Mary Jo helped him with his homework. (Refuse to believe he could manage material on his own. Too stupid. Also, too much of an opinionated jerk.)

"Courtney's from Colorado," Mary Jo said when she introduced us. They were drinking giant Sprites and going through her CD collection, playing all the really awful stuff. Which is all of it.

"Oh." He almost glared at me. Like what is wrong with Colorado??? And even if there were something he didn't like about it, how is that *my* fault? Did I discover the state?

"What's that bumper sticker?" he grunted as he pointed at the T or D one on the wall.

I told him it was a place where I used to work. In the evil state of Colorado. I said it was a really popular place to hang out. He looked confused when I described the smoothies. "It's like Dairy Queen," I finally told him. Doofus.

"I hate Dairy Queen," he said. Idiot.

"Me too," Mary Jo said. "There's not enough butter-fat in the ice cream, it tastes watered down or something."

"Well, it wasn't *like* DQ, really," I said. But there wasn't much point getting into it, not if they didn't know what I was talking about.

I left and went to the library, where I am now. If they keep dating, I will be spending a lot of time here. Which is just as well, I can ace all my classes and get my degree in 3 years.

GO AWAY. If you concentrate on something intensely enough, it will happen. Right?

Oops. Forgot crucial component of my thought.

GO AWAY, JOE.

I'm waiting. Nothing's happening. It's practically midnight, and Joe has been here since like 4:00. First he and Mary Jo were doing math homework together. So I went out for a while. When I came back, they were using my computer to look up favorite country singers' websites. Had to listen to bad songs filtered through my computer.

Went out again. Came back again.

Now he and Mary Jo are deciding what kind of pizza to order. Which means he'll be here waiting for pizza, then eating pizza . . . then I'll be listening to Joe talk about how Wisconsin pizza is so much better than Colorado pizza . . .

"So, um, Joe. Do you have a roommate?" I finally asked.

"Yeah. He's really loud, though," he said.

And you're not??? Go away!!!

Mary Jo just went to pay for pizza downstairs and I am stuck here with Joe.

"Are you writing a paper or something?" Joe grunted.

"This is my journal," I said.

"Journal?"

"Like . . . a diary," I explained. How long exactly *has* he been living in civilized society, anyway?

"Oh." He looked fairly bored. "My little sister keeps one of those. She writes all about boys. I stole it once and read the whole thing. Pretty boring."

Just as I thought, he's such a wonderful person.

JOE: If you are reading this right now?

You're too close.

GO AWAY!!!

"Maybe this isn't such a good idea," Thyme said as we marched toward the football field this morning. Her, me, the rest of the Badicals. Wittenauer couldn't be there as he was busy dancing in front of the crowd, sparring with opposing school's mascot, which was a cow, which could destroy ear of corn in seconds flat.

We set up at the CFC end of the field. I draped a banner from the uprights that said "Ozone End Zone." Yes, my brilliant idea. Thank you very much.

Whenever cheerleaders chanted "C—F—C!" we waited until they were done, then chanted, "No more C—F—C! No more C—F—C!" and "Change the name! Change the name!" Somebody had stolen some bullhorns from a gym office, so we were very loud. We interrupted the halftime show by charging across the field carrying flags and spray cans, wearing CFC sweatshirts with big circles and red lines through the initials. The one campus security guard that was working kept trying to chase us, but Corny/Wittenauer diverted her by chasing *her* instead—great comic relief, especially when she slipped on the field and fell in the mud. It was *so awesome*.

Except for one small problem.

Nobody knew what to make of us. Nobody got it.

Also, my floor seems totally split about the whole thing. Early in the game, before the football team forced us to get out of the end zone, Tricia and some other girls from the floor went by and glared at me. I heard Tricia mutter something like, "She doesn't even eat meat," and "*so* on the fringe."

But then Annemarie came over with the other half of our floor and they all high-fived me and Thyme, and said we were hilarious, so we felt better until Thyme pointed out that this wasn't supposed to be funny, it's a very, very serious issue. While she was talking, Mary Jo and Joe came walking up.

"Um, what are you guys doing?" Mary Jo asked. Like all our signs and banners didn't make it totally clear.

"This is a joke, right?" Joe asked. "Nice sweatshirts." He kept laughing at us.

"Some of us are less evolved than others," Thyme said.

"Why would I *want* to be involved in this?" Joe replied.

"Evolved. Not *involved*," I told him.

He looked at Mary Jo and they had some secret exchange and then they left. She's not home tonight. Ew.

Just got back from cafeteria. Have another protest group idea. They started this new "theme" meal-thing tonight, called Oktoberfest. Basically it's supposed to reflect German cuisine, so the bins are full of meat simmering in cabbage juice and there's potato salad with bacon bits.

Who invented bacon bits? Why do they seem like a good idea for any kind of salad? Wrong wrong wrong.

I asked how long this theme was going to go on and Larry, Caf. Supervisor, said "All month!" and I said, "Okay, but what Oktoberfest feature do you have for vegetarians?" and his smile disappeared and he said sauerkraut was a vegetable.

That's when I noticed that lots of people in the buffet line were staring at me. Pointing fingers. Should have gone to a bigger college, where no one would remember me. Should have colored my hair a boring brown, or should maybe wear large hats from now on. But that would be running away from my idea. I can't do that. I believe in what I'm doing. Even if it means that my floor is broken into factions and some people don't want me there.

When I got home, Joe was in our room. I didn't want to be there. Thyme was fighting with Kirsten. So I knocked on Annemarie's door. She turned down the music, told me to come in. I asked if I could hang for a while. She said sure, I slammed door behind me, she turned up music. Music is so loud I can barely think, let alone focus on completing sentences. It's perfect, actually.

Like dishing up glorified pigs in blankets is not bad enough! I got this ultimatum from Jennifer today re: the regimental hairnet. She found one hair in the cheddar spread and claimed it was mine because it was orange, and my hair is sort of reddish. Never mind that the cheddar is *orange*!!!

"Courtney, I'm not telling you again. Either wear your hairnet, or get your hair cut short. And don't forget to mop the ladies' restroom."

I felt like Cinderella. Mopping the ladies' while Mark/Marc sat in a stall and smoked his Benson & Hedges 100. Only consolation is that everyone gets treated the same way. Very very poorly.

Thought I had a brilliant idea today.

Need to stop having those thoughts. Wrong every time.

Thyme convinced me to get my hair cut to avoid having to wear evil hairnet, to avoid Jennifer's constant reprimands. I thought about it for a while and decided I'd look okay with short hair. "Anyway, there's power in really short hair," Thyme said, throwing in some details about I wouldn't be oppressed by society's rigid standards of beauty, etc. She made it sound like she was going to shave my head, so maybe I should have stopped right there and then. But she was being so funny, pretending to run a real beauty salon. She gave me one of her roommate's magazines to read while I sat there waiting for her to chop it off. She was getting everything ready. She said she worked one summer at a hair salon. I trusted her. Why? Couldn't I just *look* at her hundred-braid hair and realize a short cut would not be her specialty?

But I was reading the magazine and having a great time until I came upon this article: "So You and Your Boyfriend Go to Different Colleges—Can It Work?"

They had all these stats about how few LDRs survive freshman year, and who cheats first, and all these way-too-easy-to-read pie charts that caught my eye when I tried to look away. The really big pieces of pie represented the couples that didn't make it.

"This is all a bunch of crap," I said as I threw the magazine across the room.

"Oh, I know, I *hate* those magazines," Thyme said. "I just thought you might see a short hairstyle you want."

I tried to smile. But then I saw what Thyme had done to my hair, how much of it was on the floor, how little was left on my head.

If only I'd looked at the stupid celeb hair photos instead of the article that was far too relevant to my personal life. I'd still have good hair and wouldn't be depressed.

I called Grant to tell him about my new 'do. He couldn't talk for long because he has a bio exam tomorrow at 8. Quite obvious to me that his program is about 100 times more challenging than mine right now. I am stuck in Intro World. Everything's 101 and below.

Just got up to check my hair in the mirror again. "It's very, um, flattering," Mary Jo said. "It really shows off your ears."

I need new earrings. ASAP.

"Courtney, you certainly look . . . unique."

This is Dean Sobransky's idea of a compliment. Isn't he supposed to be making students feel okay about themselves?

Turned out his so-called small talk about hairstyles was just his way of stopping by my cubicle so he could ask me about what happened on Saturday. "Your little protest was, well, *unique*." Like that's the only word he knows how to use when he can't say anything nice.

"Thanks," I said. "We enjoyed it." I turned around to start dialing. Didn't even have a card ready for a person to call, but I didn't want to talk to him about my C—F—C ban idea.

He hovered by my cubicle, then actually put his hand over the thingy to hang up the phone. "But . . . er, well, of course you don't plan on continuing that," Dean S. said.

"Well . . . "

"Do you?"

"Umm . . . "

"Good. I'd hate to create such a diversion on campus . . . which could create division . . . which might lead to dissension . . ." Then he got to the real point. "Especially with Parents Weekend coming up! We need to put our best foot forward. Don't you agree?"

Totally forgot about Parents Weekend and the fact Dad has promised to come. Jotted down a note to call him before my shift was over to confirm.

Fortunately another Fun-Times Funder called Dean S. over to her cubicle just then. Wittenauer rushed over and asked if Sobransky was giving me a hard time.

"Parents Weekend is exactly why we have to keep it up, be vigilant," Corny insisted.

"Yeah, but it's different for you," I whispered. "You're in costume. You're happy *corn*. No one knows you're in on the whole thing."

"Don't give up," Wittenauer said. "We're all in this together, and we're going to make things happen here. Okay? Trust me." He rubbed my shoulder and I felt this weird pang. First human contact in 6 weeks. Okay, first *boy* contact. Hugging all the members of the food co-op when I met them doesn't count.

Went to Wanda's Wauza Beauty Shoppe this afternoon. Wanda gave me this sad look and started telling me if I wore more makeup and maybe got one of those push-up bras, maybe people wouldn't look at my hair so much. And I should come back in 3–6 months for a trim. A *trim*. Like I'll need one.

When Joe came over saw my hair today, he just laughed. And laughed. And started calling me "Truth or Hairless." Like that's even a joke. Certainly not funny. Mary Jo was laughing, too. Too afraid to stand up to him and explain that it wasn't my fault.

Tried to talk to Mary Jo today, about Joe. I think he is truly evil. Insists on calling me "Truth or Dairy Queen," which is not even a good name for a cross-dresser.

And also, I want our room back. Next thing you know he'll be sleeping over, and THAT CAN'T HAPPPEN.

So we went to breakfast together, and over dry bran cereal and a banana, I said, "Mary Jo, have you ever thought about . . . I don't know. Breaking up with Joe?"

She laughed. "Why would I want to do *that*?"

"Look at all the cute guys walking around," I said.

I should've looked up before I said that. I never realized that most hotties don't show up at the CF caf before 8 A.M. Lots of guys wearing sweats and carrying stacks of donuts do.

"Anyway, you could go out with any guy here you wanted to," I said.

"That's not true!" Mary Jo said. "Besides, I'm really happy with Joe. Why are you bringing this up? He didn't *do* anything to upset you, did he?" She looked very concerned as she buttered a butter roll.

"Oh, no. Not at all," I said. She's so sweet sometimes, it kills me. I can't just *demand* that she break up with her boyfriend. That wouldn't be fair. I can, however, continue to strongly suggest it.

Parents Weekend started tonight. Dad's coming tomorrow. Mary Jo's parents couldn't come because they're busy with a cow crisis, so 1 of her 6 brothers came—Ed. Mary Jo kept leaving us alone in the room while she went to look for Joe, who wasn't answering his phone. Joe was supposed to introduce her to his parents and then they'd all go out to dinner, but he never showed up. Mary Jo was completely devastated, not realizing that 1 meal without Joe wouldn't kill her and would only make her stronger. Maybe strong enough to dump him.

***ARE YOU READING THIS, JOE? I HOPE YOU ARE.

Anyway, Mr. Ed just sat there and stared at me, so I kept nervously talking. He kept smiling and nodding and laughing. He really needs to get out more, because I wasn't being very entertaining at all, plus I have a chopped pixie cut. I think they need to find 7 brides for 7 brothers. 6 brothers. Like, soon.

Later, after Ed finally convinced Mary Jo they should go to dinner without Joe, and after Ed made a dozen excuses for Joe in order to make MJ feel better (very sweet of him), I ran into Thyme in the hallway with her parents. She calls them "Mother" and "Father." Mother wears lots of plaid wool and expensive jewelry and calls Thyme "Morgan." Father wouldn't get off his cell phone, but did brusquely shake my hand. I think in their case the apple does fall far from the tree. Saw them pull away from dorm later in Jaguar, just as Dad was pulling up in rented mini-van. Mini-vans rule my life. Also ruin it.

Wait a second. Thyme said her family had lost all their money. So how can they drive a brand-new Jag?

Work today was insanely busy. You don't want to know
how many visiting parents want Knockwurst Knots for
breakfast. Bluck. Shudder. Etc.

"This place is making so much money, it's disgusting," Mark/Marc/now Marque said as he shoved a wad
of twenties into the safe. "The register is like overflow-
ing. And we're making six seventy-five an hour? I don't
think so."

"Yeah, but we get these *aprons*," Ben pointed out.
Marque has decorated his with a large button that says
"Have a Day." "So Courtney, are you going to be doing
your halftime show?" he teased me.

I've been trying to convince Ben and Marque to join
our group, because we could use more members, especially ones that I'm already friends with. But they're not
convinced yet. Marque won't wear heinous CFC sweatshirts, even if it's to protest them. Ben is more interested
in his slightly more respectable Political Debate Union
group, which I would probably check out were I not so
deeply embroiled in the CFC protest already.

Anyway, we were completely thwarted at the football
game today. Dean Sobransky, or someone else in charge,
had hired multiple security guards to surround campus,
ring off football field, and prevent us from making our
point. No halftime show. No radical Badicals presence at
the game, though most of our people did wear the sweatshirts with the red line through CFC.

"What we have here is a case of Protestus Inter-ruptus," co-Badical Erik said when we all met under the goalposts before the game (I had told Dad a little about what was happening, but not much). "We might get a lot of publicity, but we might just look really, really bad." Also, we all had to admit that the group was about ¼ the size it usually was, due to people hanging out with their parents.

I guess it was just as well, because I had my hands full with Dad. And then some. First off—he had to bring Angelina's baby with him, because Angelina has the flu and so does her mom, Dad's new wife, Sophia (not to be confused with Mary Jo's cow Sophie). (Can I get a *chart* with this?) Nobody where they live could baby-sit, and Dad's all of a sudden Mr. Grandparent of the Year, so he decided to bring her along, all the way from Arizona.

I have nothing against babies. I might have one, in like 10 or 15 years. But Bellarina isn't just any baby. She's the loudest baby in existence. And being away from her mom and grandma definitely wasn't helping. So far, Mary Jo is the only one here who can get Bellarina to calm down. Wanted her to come with us but of course she had to hang out with Ed and look for Joe, who had once again mysteriously disappeared.

Dad, Bellarina, and I sat in the bleachers. Started out next to Thyme and her parents. At first Bellarina was being cute. I sat there with her on my lap and watched Corny Wittenauer posing for photos in front of the bleachers, wrapping his cornstalk arms around students as moms and dads positioned cameras.

Then suddenly it all went horribly wrong: Bellarina screaming, Thyme's mom and dad casting many aggravated looks, people from different classes of mine scowling at me, Dad trying to put Bellarina's binky in her mouth, Bellarina throwing it at Thyme's mom with so much baby spit on it that it stuck to her blond coiffed hair. Thyme's parents insisting they move; Thyme insisting that Bellarina simply needed a calming environment; taking Bellarina and leaving bleachers to sit under tree; Dad and I trying to ignore screams and cries becoming louder and louder.

End result: Thyme and her parents bought tickets and went to sit in the Preferred Parents' enclosed Plexiglas booths section.

Bellarina decided it was time to become stinky while sucking her binky. So it was off to the restroom to change her. But then Dad had to go back into the bathroom afterward, so he asked if I would hold her. Which I was doing, and she wasn't even screaming, so I thought things were looking up. Until Dean Sobransky came along. I thought he might be about to thank me for not staging a major protest, but his face turned all red when he saw me. Very embarrassed.

"Well, er, Courtney," he said. "How old is your, ah, she?"

"Oh, um . . . " I had to think. "About a year, I guess. No, wait. Ten months."

He seemed sort of surprised that I didn't know,

exactly. Then he bolted into the men's room and that was the end of it. Very weird guy. Can't talk about much except "college's best interests."

Later on, Bellarina finally went to sleep in the hotel suite, so Dad and I ordered in calzones (mine without cheese), which is what we always do together, and sat around talking. Somehow, God help me, we got on the topic of "my relationship."

"Courtney, you'll find out a lot about Grant in the year you're apart."

"Years, Dad," I said. "It's going to be four *years*."

"Oh." He rubbed the side of his nose. "Well. That's a long time. Who knows what will happen." He made it sound incredibly tragic, like we were doomed. And maybe we are. And if we are, it's all my fault. I could have stayed home. Why was it so important for me to go 1,000 miles away? Just because Alison did it, in the opposite direction, and I must always copy her? Because I didn't want to live at home and knew Mom would make me? Because I was afraid I'd be stuck in same rut, with same job, same friends, forever?

Nothing wrong with ruts. Wagons would never have crossed plains without them.

Then again, if wagons hadn't crossed the plains, buffalo would still be around in the thousands and millions, not fighting for existence.

But then I might not exist.

Going to sleep now. Must stop this wagon train of thought immediately.

Finally got up the nerve to tell Dad over our good-bye brunch that I needed some extra spending money because my credit card limit wasn't very high and I might be getting sort of near it. I said it while Bellarina was screaming and banging her spoon and throwing food, so that I'd seem like the good child, the easy child. We visited a Tyme machine before they left for the airport. I came home with $200 and scrambled eggs in my hair.

Very exciting news in cafeteria tonight. The student association is chartering a bus to take anyone who wants to cough up $20 to Madison next weekend—we'll leave Saturday morning, come back Sunday at noon. Hurray! I'm going to see Jane! When I called to tell her, she was totally excited.

Grant called tonight. It was really fun because I kept making him laugh even though he doesn't really know Dad (except for hanging out at graduation party) or Thyme and her snooty parents or anyone in the Ozone End Zone group. At the end of our talk he said, "I'm really proud of you, Courtney. It sounds like things are going really well." Afterward I realized he hadn't said much about his weekend. Was it good? Bad? Indifferent? What did he do? I don't remember. Did he say? Did I monopolize the entire conversation? Maybe I should call back. But I have too much homework left to do before tomorrow.

Can't believe what happened at work today. First, a group of men from some office all came in at the same time to order meat rolls, kept asking me what my favorite menu item was, kept making "knock knock" jokes, asked me if I thought the Brat Blankets were as good as the bacon bit Bacles.

"Sure," I said. "They're . . . wonderful." If you like food involving casing, that makes you think of meat grinders, and slaughterhouses.

Oh God. Just realized something. Grandpa would be so happy if he knew I was in charge of the Best Wurst Bagels Ever team. All those years of lecturing me and showing me barbecue techniques for keeping burgers pink and juicy while at the same time killing *E. coli*. . . . Meanwhile I was trying not to spew on the lawn figurines. It was all actually paying off. Disgustingly.

Anyway, finally got the annoying guys through the line when Dean Sobransky came in. Either he'd just heard about our exciting new menu (and it's true, the line has gone out the door for these Brat Blankets) or he was continuing his plan to spy on me and watch my every move and turn me in to campus authorities before I succeed in changing the school name.

I guess Dean S. didn't know I worked there and was very surprised to see me. So he ordered a few items and started stammering something about how my BF job must help me "make ends meet," with "your little one at home to consider."

"What? You have a baby?" Mark/Marc/Marque asked. "How adorable."

"You never mentioned that. I thought you lived in the dorm," Ben said. Looking totally shocked and defrauded.

My face burning. Me trying to pretend it was because I was standing too close to steam table. "I *do* live in the dorm," I said. "And I don't have a baby."

"But I saw you on Saturday. And you know, it's appropriate for students to be parents as well as children. And—oh, she's the spitting image of Courtney," Dean S. went on.

"That's because she's my dad's stepdaughter's—wait a second, we're not even related by blood. She doesn't look anything like me!"

"Courtney, what's this I hear? You're a single mom?" Jennifer asked as she rushed over to horn in on the conversation from hell. "You never mentioned that! You need family health insurance coverage, you need company-credit day care, you need some of our bagel teething rings—"

"No! My stepsister. *She* has a baby," I explained. "My dad brought her—the baby—for Parents Weekend, because my stepsister was home sick, and *that's* who you saw me holding."

Jennifer and Ben and Marque all stared at me, like they were trying to figure out if I was telling the truth or not.

"Guys! If I had a baby, don't you think I would have mentioned her by now?" I asked.

"Um. Well. No," Dean S. murmured.

"See, people here don't really, um, talk about stuff like that," Jennifer said. "Which is okay!"

People here are so weird.

Can I leave for Madison tonight? I am so embarrassed! There was an article about me in the school paper today, about the CFC protest last week (yes, the paper's notoriously slow about getting the word out) (or maybe Dean S. made them "hold the story" until now?). There was even a little picture of me, leading the chant. Why couldn't they use my school ID photo when I had hair, when I was vaguely attractive? Then again, real politicians don't think about these things. I should really be more serious about this.

"Next time you're getting your picture in the paper, you should really let me give you a makeover," said Julie, a girl on the hall, when I saw her in the cafeteria. "I used to work at a cosmetics counter."

"Oh?" My voice wavered as I realized she was really insulting me.

"I'm only saying that because I want you to win. I once set my sister's hair on fire by using hairspray in an aerosol can while I was smoking," she said. "Those cans are so dangerous, they definitely should be banned."

1. We clearly need to better explain what our cause is.
2. I won't ever let her give me a makeover.

LATER...

Just got back from taking a shower. When I went in, Tricia was standing at sink, brushing her teeth with battery-powered toothbrush. I said hi, trying to be civil. Which was useless. She gave me the cold shoulder, like I'm all of a sudden a terrible, horrible person, because I want to get rid of CFC sweatshirts. Oh yes. I really *should* do some jail time for that.

Then I had turned off the shower but I was still standing in the shower stall, drying off, when I heard Gretchen and Peña come in and discuss how the school was even more political than they'd hoped, how they admired me for taking a stand, and how everyone needs to get involved at a grass roots level. (Does that include a grass football-field level?)

Then I was walking down the hall when I heard Tricia telling Brittany and Kirsten how "It's like, I don't know how it's like where she's, like, from? But Courtney has no like *morals*?"

Never knew I could cause so much controversy.

Dean S. made his usual visit to our hallowed cubicles this afternoon. He was wearing giant snow boots and kept stopping to ask everyone if they'd taken precautions for the coming freak winter storm. Seemed in a holly-jolly mood to me. Or he was, until he saw me.

"Courtney, I forgot you worked on Wednesdays," he said, his face getting that purplish look again.

Does he have a crush on me or something? No, impossible. But that's how he acts sometimes. Too uncomfortable to be alive.

So he mentioned the *CF Courier* article about me and asked did I really mean what I said?

"Um, what did I say?" I asked. Because I barely remembered the reporter interviewing me. In fact I don't think she did. She's a member of the group and just sort of roughly quoted us.

"That no school today should be allowed to have the initials of a banned substance," Dean S. said. "Do you really believe that?"

"Well," I said, racking my brain. "You don't see schools with the initials DDT. Or TCE. Or even PCP."

"I think you mean PCB," Dean S. said.

"Right. Whatever," I said.

"No, but—but—" Dean S. sputtered as he tossed his leather gloves up to the ceiling and caught them. "We're talking about a reputation. We're talking about a hundred and thirty-seven years of history," he said.

"And we're talking about destroying the ozone layer and promoting things that contribute to that," I said.

Then it got ugly.

Dean S. shoved his gloves into his pocket and came closer to me. "Weren't you interested in transferring at one point?" he asked. "Because I'm not sure you're going to be happy here, Courtney. And I could get you accepted at another college with a good reputation. I could find you a financial offer."

It was like getting threatened by the Mafia! "You mean, an offer I couldn't refuse?" I asked. I couldn't believe it. Dean S. wanted to get rid of me. I didn't know whether to be scared, or just damn impressed with myself. I was an instigator!

Then Wittenauer wheeled over in his chair. "You know, Dean Sobransky, you've always been so supportive of an open discussion of the issues. I'm really surprised to hear you talk that way. What's going on?" School mascot was completely coming to my rescue.

Dean S. cleared his throat. "Well, Walter, it's like this."

I nearly fell out of my cubicle. Walter Wittenauer? And I thought I had it bad with my V.D. initials? My life was *cake*. No wonder he was hiding under a mascot costume!

Dean S. and WW got into an in-depth discussion of issues facing Cornwall Falls, universities in general, the world. I joined in whenever it seemed appropriate. Ended with one of those famous statements that never made any sense to me, that we'd all "agree to disagree."

Still, have to look over my shoulder, make sure Dean S. isn't trying to boot me out of school.

I don't believe this. When I got back from class this morning, hiking through snowdrifts, Mary Jo, earliest riser of them all, was still in bed. She was crying. I asked her what was wrong. She said Joe broke up with her. That idiot! Joe, I mean. Like he can do better than Mary Jo! He should be grateful she spent even one day with him, let alone a month or so. And the worst part of all is the stuff he said to her when he did it. He told her that he wasn't attracted to her anymore, because she was sort of overweight. What?! She is not! And maybe he could have thought of that before ordering extra cheese and meat on every pizza they ever ordered. I'm so furious! I want to kill him. But I don't believe in killing, or at least I thought I didn't—until now. She's *not* overweight, and even if she were, she's a great person, if you like that kind of person, so who cares?

"I'm going to call Ed and your other brothers right now. They can come down tonight and kick Joe's butt." I grabbed the telephone. I also made Mary Jo look outside at the pretty snow and drink hot chocolate I made for her. "What's your home number?"

"What? Don't call them!" Mary Jo said.

"But you have to. Just imagine them showing up at his dorm room." I stared at her family portrait, all the tall, beef-raised guys perched on a giant tractor. "They'd stand in the doorway and he'd probably faint. It would be so perfect."

"But they wouldn't come just to do that," Mary Jo said.

"Sure they would!" I told her. "Big brothers are way into sticking up for their little sisters. Not that I know, but I've seen my little brother stand up for me. Anyway, all they'd have to do is carry something dangerous. Like a farm knife or something."

"A *farm* knife? What's that?" Mary Jo laughed.

"That's not important. The key thing is to make him as miserable as he's making *you*," I said.

Mary Jo just sat there looking at me like a scared bunny rabbit. That's when I realized that she didn't have a sister or a best friend like Beth, and didn't understand how these things were done. You get furious together, you plot revenge, you talk about things you're never ever going to actually say or do.

"He's right, you know," she said, sounding pathetic. "I should probably go on a diet."

"What? But you're not overweight!" I said.

"I am," Mary Jo said. "Look, I've got farmer's flab." She pinched her waist. There was like one millionth of an inch of extra skin.

"Mary Jo. You're being ridiculous," I said. "He was trying to think of some dumb reason he could use to break up with you. That's what they always do."

"They do? How many guys have you gone out with?"

I was giving her the impression that I was quite the skank, I guess. I explained that I wasn't a skank, but that I'd gone through one bad breakup and had seen a bunch more.

Mary Jo looked at me blankly. "Skank? Is that like the past tense of skunk?" she asked, and we both cracked up laughing.

But then Mary Jo started crying again about 2 minutes later and I really needed to think of some way to cheer her up. Field trip to Farm Supply? Buy her a new mane comb? Kill Joe for her?

Grant called tonight and after I talked to him for a while, he talked to Mary Jo for a couple of minutes. She told me what he said—he was being super-nice to Mary Jo on account of her heartache and the fact she's so blue. (She has been playing sad CDs all day, and I'm starting to talk like Martina McBride.)

He really can be so sweet. He can talk to anyone. While they were talking, I remembered when he helped me after Dave dumped me last year, how he listened to me babble about hating all guys and how they were all scum. And he didn't even take it personally.

7:00 P.M. Mom just called. Extremely frantic. Her book club is meeting at the house, and Oscar ran away when the house got too full of strangers. (He has set limits. 7 is fine; 8 is terrifying.) She hasn't found him yet, and Bryan isn't home because he's out with Beth, they're studying together.

I got so jealous of Beth and how she still gets to be with her boyfriend, even if it is my brother. I wonder how it would be if Grant and I got to study together. We probably wouldn't get enough done. So okay, we'd just hang together for an hour or so, like a sort of pre-study or post-study thing, and—

"Courtney!" Mom said. "Are you listening to me? What am I going to do about Oscar?"

"He'll come back," I predicted. "He's probably hiding under the bushes in Mr. Novotny's yard. Go check."

Mom walked outside with the phone and called him. Nothing. "Oh, I wish Grant were still around," she said. "I could really use him right now."

"Mom," I said. "Don't even tell *me* about needing Grant, okay?"

Well, at least I made her laugh.

I've got to leave for the movies now.

LATER ...

Mom just called back. She found Oscar. Actually she and this guy Richard from her book club, the one who's in love with her, only Mom doesn't care, found him. Richard is this really, really nice guy who won't pick a book when it's his turn unless Mom also likes the book. And he insists on bringing food to the house whenever it's Mom's turn to host. Richard = total devotion. Mom = total insanity. The guy is good-looking, about 50, and as far as I can tell is bucks-up. What is the deal with that? Mom would rather get involved in a torrid chat-room affair. I sent her a clipping about a murder where a wife hooked up with a guy on the Internet; husband followed wife to the motel where they were meeting, shot everyone including himself. All Mom said was that it didn't apply to her because she wasn't married anymore.

Meanwhile, I went to this French film, part of on-campus foreign film series. Dreadful, depressing, subtitles. Felt intelligent. Felt really bored, also. Afterward Thyme insisted on discussing it. I had to pretend I'd actually watched the whole thing instead of sitting there daydreaming about going to movies this past summer with Grant, and daydreaming about leaving town tomorrow for Madison. Can't wait to see Jane. Can't wait to be around other people.

"Courtney, you've lost weight! You're so skinny!"

That was the first thing Jane said when I got out of the van at the UW Student Union, staggering a little because I'd been scrunched up in the back.

"Look—you're not even strong enough to walk!" Jane said.

"I am, too," I said as I gave her a big hug. Then I explained what happened: the bus didn't show up like it was supposed to. We had 2 cargo vans, and that was it. People were literally fighting for seats, until they decided to have a lottery. I don't think I've ever prayed so hard for anything in my life, except maybe that they wouldn't serve chicken at my graduation party. So they'd given away almost all the seats except for this one in the way, way back—and that was mine. Practically under the luggage.

Jane said the first thing we had to do—after lunch—was go find some clothes in my actual size at the thrift shop. I guess I hadn't noticed, but now that I'm back in civilized society, and Jane has a full-length mirror, I guess I am looking sort of like a 14-year-old boy with my baggy look and short hair. "You're like a stick. Haven't you been eating?" Jane asked.

"Sure," I said. It was just that the cafeteria pickings for vegetarians are woefully slim. But I supplemented. Constantly. "Of course I've been eating, Jane, don't be ridiculous." But when I thought about it, not that much, really, except Twizzlers, plain bagels, and chocolate soy-milk. Hm. Maybe I am a 14-year-old boy.

Jane took me to an Indian restaurant. All delicious. All stuff that I absolutely couldn't get in Wauzataukie. Felt like I was in heaven, or at least a colder facsimile of Boulder. We drank coffee, talked and talked, walked up and down State Street, bought cheap earrings and cool boots, and then Jane drove me to this place called Ella's, where she insisted I order something called the #1. Turned out to be a pound cake sundae, with vanilla ice cream and hot fudge and whipped cream. "Jane," I said. "You know I can't eat this."

"I saw you eat a banana split this summer at work," Jane reminded me. "So break your rules again—do it for me, Courtney. We have to fatten you up."

"I'm not a cow," I said. She made me sound like I was getting ready for the slaughterhouse and wouldn't fetch a good price at auction.

"You're not anorexic or something dumb like that, are you?" Jane asked as she stirred sugar into her coffee. "Because we all made a pledge to each other that we'd never go down that road." She hit her spoon against the table. "Oh, no. I forgot how bad you are at keeping your pledges."

"I am not," I protested, as my mouth literally watered.

But Jane looked really worried. And the sundae looked really good. But I couldn't, I told her. But then I did.

And it was delicious.

Perhaps it's time to reevaluate my survival strategy.

Instead of being vegan, I could be a lacto-vegetarian. Let's face it, eggs and milk are easier to find around here than alfalfa and seaweed.

"Anyway, I'm not bad at pledges," I told Jane. "Grant and I pledged to make our relationship work, no matter what. And we're doing it."

"Mm." Jane took a sip of coffee but didn't say much else.

"What?" I asked. "Our relationship is surviving just fine."

She stared at these little Beatles marionette things that were dancing around, near the ceiling.

"Aren't we?" I asked, waving my spoon in front of her face. "Or do you know something I don't?"

"Hey, I don't know anything," Jane said. "I just think it's kind of unrealistic to assume you can be exclusive for an entire year when you're not together. Your relationship might be fine," she said. "But are *you*?"

I might have just been getting woozy from the sundae, but it sounded like she was being really critical. Of me and Grant. What's to criticize? Not me. Not Grant. So is there something else I should know about or worry about?

JANE HERE:
Hi, journal. Haven't talked to you lately, but want you to keep an eye on your owner/creator. Very worried about Courtney. Short hair, gaunt, looks pale. Wonder if it's because she misses Grant? Romantic, but stupid (sorry, Court, but *you*

151

come first). Or it could just be major Vitamin D deficiency; no milk, no sun. Well, either way, Courtney, you need to put on some pounds. You're supposed to gain the freshman fifteen, not *lose* it. Very worried about Beth, also. She goes out almost every night, cracked up her mother's car that one time, is getting D's in her classes, and on top of all that is not being very nice to Bryan.

I never even saw Jane write in here. How funny.

Unfortunately I'm back from Madison. Had a great time with Jane and new bf Charles and saw his band and everything. But now I'm back in the land of total disasters.

While I was gone, Joe came over yesterday and brought Mary Jo flowers and told her she was beautiful and skinny, and I get the impression he spent the night, ew, and now they're off on a date at Il Fromaggio. Boy can tell her to lose weight and then take her out for lasagna and breadsticks. Like a couple of multicultural carnations make up for the way he insulted her and broke it off out of the blue. Multi*colored* carnations, whatever. I feel like going to the restaurant and spying on him, making sure he doesn't say something about he just realized what he was missing, blah blah blah. If I had his cell phone number I'd call it and tell him there was an emergency at home.

I just know he's only doing this because he misses her, or he needs something from her—not because he cares.

"Courtney, you don't know that," Grant said when I called him to complain. "He might have the best intentions."

"They have a giant midterm coming up," I said. "His intention is to pass bio. And Mary Jo can help him do it."

"You're shortchanging Mary Jo," Grant said. "Don't

you think he might miss her? She seems like a really great person, and you said she's cute, so . . . why wouldn't he want her back?"

There it is again. That Mary Jo worship tone.

"The question isn't about Mary Jo," I said. "The thing is that Joe is a heinous individual and can't be trusted."

"You're too hard on people, you know that?" Grant said. He sounded sort of critical. How dare he? He's not here, he doesn't know Joe. If he met him for even 2 seconds, he'd hate him. But suddenly I'm the one who's critical?

"Yeah, sure. Whatever. I have to go to the library," I said, and rushed off the phone. Stupid Joe is now ruining Mary Jo's life, and my life with Grant as well.

Mary Jo and I got into a huge fight this morning because I told her that Joe was only using her. She said he wasn't and that I was really mean to say that, and only someone as "jaded and skanky" as me would have such an evil thought.

Jaded and skanky? Sounds like a kids' show. 2 new dwarves have been added to "Snow White": Jaded and Skanky! Oh—don't forget Critical. I'm just getting so many compliments lately, I can hardly keep track of them all.

Can I help it if I've gone on a *few* more dates than Mary Jo? Which isn't her fault. And it isn't my fault. She should trust me when it comes to Joe.

Want him to drop out of this school and stop ruining Mary Jo's life, and, by transitive property, my life. I hope he flunks out. Soon. Sometimes I feel like I am more involved in their relationship than my own. But that's because theirs is in town and mine isn't. Where is mine, exactly?

Mary Jo and I are talking again. Or rather, we were, for about 3 minutes. Mary Jo aced her bio midterm yesterday; Joe didn't. So after they got their midterms back, he broke up with her again.

Mary Jo very upset. So upset that she mistakenly started talking to me again; forgot about silent treatment.

I tried not to say "I told you so," but I'm not very good at that. I have this thing where I just really really enjoy being right. Except that I wasn't enjoying it, because Mary Jo started crying again. Whatever I said came out totally wrong, and she went out of the room and slammed the door behind her.

"What was that all about?" Thyme asked, coming across the hall. Behind her, loud reggae music blared. "There is way too much hostility around here. I think it's because of the asbestos in the carpeting."

"No, it isn't," I said. "There's nothing wrong with this dorm! Except the people in it." Then I slammed the door in her face. I really don't know what came over me.

Oh crap. Now Thyme hates me. Mary Jo hates me. Krystyne came by, pretending she wanted to "chat," but was fishing for information to fill out her weekly "conflict report" to the housing office.

Mary Jo is on a hunger strike. I went to get a fruit juice from the fridge tonight, and discovered the cupboard is bare. Completely. "What happened to all the food in here?" I asked.

"Oh, I got rid of it all," she said.

For a split second I wondered if she ate it all. One of those breakup-induced binges. But she said she threw it out because her sponsor told her to remove temptation from her life.

"Sponsor?" I asked. "Temptation?"

She's joined some on-campus group that makes it sound like dieting is a religion.

"How about if you just sort of cut back?" I suggested. "You only have like five pounds to lose, at most. At most! And you look fine anyway and shouldn't worry about what Joe said."

"Easy for you to say," Mary Jo grumbled. "You've dropped at least ten pounds since we got here *and* you have a terrific guy back home waiting for you." She made it sound like we were off at war together, sharing a bunker.

Then she showed me all these brochures from this weight-loss group. Scary. She's convinced she'll get Joe back if she does this. Should I throw this stuff out so it can't work?

Meanwhile, I'm supposed to be organizing this giant rally for Saturday, have to meet with the group tomorrow. Need new ideas.

Where is Grant when I need him? Not home again. Left a message. Just got back from huge party at Mark/Marc/Marque's house. One of his roommates has it every fall, and it's called the "Oshkosh Slosh," because he's from Oshkosh and so are a bunch of people here. I didn't get sloshed, but I did dance a lot. Maybe a little sloshed, earlier, but switched over to water 3 glasses ago.

Funny thing happened. Was talking to Marque about Grant and how much I miss Grant and so he asked if I had a picture. Which I do in my wallet. Crumpled but still cute. So I was showing it to him and he was totally impressed. Marque and I sat on the stairs and talked for an hour about relationships and how hard they are and how great they are, etc.

Then Marque asked if I worry about Grant being with other women, because after all he is hot. Marque said if he dated Grant he wouldn't let him out of his sight. I thought that was very funny so I kept laughing. Then suddenly it wasn't funny and I was almost crying. Then Marque hugged me and said just because he was paranoid and insecure didn't mean I had to be.

Then a bunch of Badicals showed up and we all danced and I forgot about missing Grant. At one point I did tipsily harass Wittenauer about his first name, and he said as if his initials weren't bad enough, he was also a 3. What? I asked. He's a lot cuter than that, I thought. Why was he rating himself only a 3?

Then he cracked up laughing and said he had a 3 at the end of his name. Like Junior, but a III. So his initials are actually WW III. Can you even believe that?

"I'm surprised you can spend so much time trying to change the college name," I said. "Don't you want to spend all your time changing your *own* initials?"

"Is there a group for that?" he asked. "Do you want to organize one?"

"Actually, yeah," I said. "But I'll tell you my middle initials some other time."

What a fun party. I really need to go to more parties.

I have decided not to drink at any more parties. Or drink anymore at parties. Or even go to parties. Not fun.

Have a major headache, still, and lost my wallet last night. I have no idea where. Completely irresponsible of me. I've retraced my steps—well, okay, so I can't remember every single step. I'm not Thyme. She did use her photographic memory to go through all the routes we walked together.

Funny how easy it was to make up with Mary Jo and Thyme. Perhaps Thyme's photographic memory is failing and she doesn't remember me shutting the door in her face?

I skimmed the Lost & Found section of the paper, and I've been to every Lost & Found desk there is.

"A wallet? Er, no," everyone said, trying not to laugh, as if everyone knows that no one ever turns in stolen wallets.

It's not like I had much in there.

Just my entire *life history*. My complete identity.

Feel very weird about hanging out and laughing with Corny last night. Like I did something wrong, had too much fun or something, and now must be punished.

Which is why Krystyne just came by and told me I had to go to a housing workshop tomorrow at 1 P.M. Mandatory.

Housing office called it "So You Got Off on the Wrong Foot: A Remedial Roommate Workshop."

I called it "Three Hours of My Life—Gone."

Mary Jo and I were there, along with Thyme and Kirsten and about 50 other miserable-looking students. Housing office won't let you move, but will spend time and money to force you to get along?

We had to do all these really stupid exercises to rebuild trust. Then we were supposed to turn to each other and each person got 2 minutes of "freestyle open expression." I went first, and I didn't even talk for 2 minutes, and if I did, it was all about Joe and what a bad choice he was for Mary Jo and how I wanted to protect her from him.

Mary Jo then started her rant and couldn't stop. She said, "No wonder you want to change the school's name. You don't agree with *anything*. You think everything should be one way, *your way*, and when it's not, you decide it's wrong," blah blah blah. I stopped listening, which was a mistake, because part of the exercise required repeating back what she had said.

"You never listen!" Mary Jo cried. "That's another thing that drives me crazy."

We left there with a giant 3-ring binder called "Cope, Don't Mope." And some extra credit that has to count *some*where.

There was some mail waiting for me today. Not the good kind. The kind that comes from the bank when your account is overdrawn. Well, of course it is, I thought—my *wallet* was stolen, my *Tyme card* was stolen—I'd already called the bank to report this, so I'm not responsible.

I went down to the bank to talk with a customer service rep. Unfortunately I got the same cranky woman who couldn't spell my middle name and lectured me on balancing my checkbook and not bouncing checks. "I was just about to call you, Ms. Vun Dragoon Smith," she said. Like I was about to make her day, because she could get all her bitchiness out in one customer transaction and then go home early. I tried to explain that the checks had bounced because someone stole my Tyme card. I told her I'd never actually written a bad check.

"Do you understand the *concept* of checking at all?" she said, as if I were 7 years old. "Listen, you are in big trouble here with us. And I warned you, didn't I?"

"But don't you see? We're dealing with a case of identity theft," I said. "Didn't you see that Sandra Bullock movie?" I explained how easy it was to have someone take your name, everything about you, and start acting like you, and start spending money like you—

Then she went to a file and came back with my signature card, and also photocopies of the bounced checks. They were all ones I'd written myself. A few of them while slightly impaired, apparently. Couldn't quite make out who they were to. It had nothing to do with my Tyme card.

"I'm sorry. Your account has been closed. Permanently," she said. "And you owe us two hundred dollars in fees."

Then she smiled. Yeah, she's so *sorry*. She lives for this.

Excellent news. Marque found my wallet at his house!
Took him out to Koffee Kitchen to celebrate. After we
ordered I realized I had no cash. Had to ask him to cover
the meal. Very embarrassing. Now owe him 2 lunches.

Called Grant on the sly from Funders today. Told him
about finding my wallet and joked how Marque was only
keeping it because he thought Grant's photo was cute.
He didn't even *laugh*. He was all preoccupied with something.

When I hung up the phone I felt vaguely insulted.
Like it wasn't exciting to hear from me?

Went over to find Wittenauer, but he was wrapped up
in a call to some former senator, discussing the needs of
higher education.

What about *my* needs?

Mental breakdown. Sampled one of our Brat Blankets and a Knockwurst Knot today. I should have known it was only a matter of time, after all I do have this weakness for hot dogs. Also I'm completely broke and need free protein.

Anyway. They were actually almost yummy. Delicious. Way better than Oscar's cheapo hot dogs.

Sorry, body.

Sorry, PETA.

Sorry, cow somewhere, pig, whatever.

It's just that everyone was talking about how good they were, and they did smell good, and . . . well, there's no *excuse*, really. And I did pay for it afterward because my stomach went into a panic. So I don't think I should be criticized, especially not in my very own journal, so just *back off*.

Wow. Meat really brings out the testosterone in me. I'm yelling at a notebook.

Afterward I was hanging out with Thyme in student coffeehouse. She kept talking about how healthy she's felt ever since she purified her body, and I was sitting there listening to rumbling of digesting bratwurst.

Why do I have this capacity to just toss my convictions aside when a situation gets too difficult? I'm really not a credit to the cause. To *any* cause.

Must revise earlier statements about cows. Turns out they are much smarter than I thought. Also somewhat vindictive.

I went for a bike ride this afternoon. There's this bike path on the outskirts of town, so I thought I'd check it out now that weather has warmed up, snow has melted. Also I've been feeling very flabby from eating too much junk food, too much meat, not enough fruit unless you count fruit roll-ups.

So I was riding along—sunny afternoon, rapidly turning cloudy, but trying to ignore that. The path turned so that it was sandwiched between 2 cow pastures. Cows seemed cute to me. Lounging, gnawing on grass, etc. Then I turned a corner and a cow was standing right in front of me. It had somehow escaped from the pasture.

Decided to ride past; wasn't going to let 1 Holstein get in my way. Kept going. Suddenly 3 cows in front of me. Then 2 more. Farther ahead, cows standing in a line, barring bike path. Giant hole in barbed-wire fence suddenly very obvious.

Cows seeking revenge on me! Bad karma from eating meat yesterday.

"I'm sorry!" I yelled. "I'm really, really sorry. It won't happen again!"

Cows ignored apology. Well, of course they would—it was a bratwurst, not a hamburger. Started coming toward me. Turned and sprinted back past 1 lonely cow that started cantering beside me, hooves clicking on bike path, my heart pounding in my throat. Courtney vs. Cows. Felt like Lance Armstrong as I raced all the way back to campus. But much, much slower.

From now on, no eating meat. Or maybe no riding bike in the country. To get cow karma back, I will only say nice things about milk, cheese, cottage cheese, sour cream, ice cream. All dairy products are bright and beautiful. And dairy cows rule.

Next time I need to at least bring some carrots or hay or whatever it is cows like to eat. But that might make them chase me more. Probably not a good idea.

So to make amends, Thyme and I went to fish fry at Brat Wurstenburger tonight. I'd heard it was a popular Friday-night thing, but didn't realize—the place was *packed*. Thyme kept asking our server, named Dot, whether the fish had come from polluted waters and whether they were actually fresh. Dot got this little eye twitch as she listened to Thyme, but kept answering her politely, telling her the perch came from lakes nearby, she knew all the fishermen who caught them—

"Fisher*people*, you mean," Thyme said.

"I've known them for years, two of them are my sons, and they're named Steve, Eric, John, and Wayne," Dot said curtly.

"She didn't have to be so rude about it," Thyme complained after Dot left. Like Thyme hadn't been as rude as possible herself.

Ozone End Zone Rules!

We blew them away at Homecoming.

Thyme unfortunately missed the whole thing because she wasn't feeling well, or so she said. Later on, she wasn't home, so I don't know. Sometimes I think she is afraid of the spotlight. Anyway, not important. What's important is this: we got *applause*. We're starting to have people who *cheer* for us, we almost have a following.

It was really cool because Annemarie convinced a friend of hers from the campus radio station (she has her own DJ slot now) to blast music over the field speakers as we dashed through 35-member marching band's lame halftime routine, disrupting everything, drawing attention to the plight of our school being associated with, well, plight. Or do I mean blight?

Anyway, the crowd was *huge*. Several old fogies in plaid pants frowning at us. Several alumni heard reminiscing about life in the sixties. Meanwhile Corny was sprinting around trying to distract Dean S., president, football coach, marching band conductor, etc. Very busy mascot. His cornsilk was falling out all over the place; looked nearly bald at the end.

Just as I was leaving the field, Dean S. caught up with me. "Courtney, I thought you'd given up on all this," he said. "Don't you want to join a—a—team or something? You seem athletic. You could channel all that energy into, say, volleyball, or field hockey—or how about tennis?

I'm the assistant coach, you know."

See, sometimes I think he does have a crush on me. Wants to be around me constantly. Very embarrassing because it looked to other Badicals like I was colluding with the enemy. "Let's agree to agree that I'm no good at tennis," I said, before running off to distribute flyers.

Shouldn't have run. He'll force me to be on the cross-country team now.

After the game we all got together to brainstorm ideas for final football game, 2 weeks from today. Everyone wants to do a dramatic scene, or okay, maybe that's just the people from the drama department who recently joined the group.

"So this would be Shakespeare in the parking lot?" Erik joked.

Looked for Wittenauer to laugh with, then remembered he had to go to various alumni functions, mingle, pose for more photos, pretend he wasn't in on this. Meeting very boring without him or Thyme there.

Forget CFC thing. Forget everything! Grant called this morning with the best news. He got me a plane ticket!!! I'm going to see him next weekend!!!

He's been working all these extra hours to save the money. Not telling me about it. And he kept asking me questions about my classes, like when my midterms were, and made me mail him a schedule, and all my dumb syllabuses. I thought he was just trying to be involved. Turns out he's been plotting this.

Best boyfriend ever. Confirmed yet again.

Ran across hall to tell Thyme the great news.

"Maybe I can come with you next weekend," Thyme said. "I have got to get out of here."

I smiled a little, hoping she wasn't serious. Don't really want to spend weekend with Grant *and* Thyme. With Grant and anyone, actually.

I've got the worst stomachache. I'm too excited about seeing Grant to do anything but think about seeing Grant. I know this is wrong because I need to get ahead on my schoolwork because I won't do any while I'm home. But instead I spent the afternoon shopping for perfect gift to bring. Ended up in Karl's House of Meat getting badgered by man behind the counter to sample latest cheese crop.

"The thing is, I don't really *like* cheese," I said. "This is a gift for a friend—"

"You'll love it after you try this!" He carved a giant chunk of something slightly stinky and handed it to me. "Now *that's* a cheese."

Well, it was either a cheese or a moldy ball of aged butter. Chunk after chunk kept coming over the counter on a wooden board. (Should really not think of chunks right now.) Ate some, stuffed some of it in my pockets, finally ended up buying a gift basket, which includes something called a "Nutted Three-Cheese Log." It's stuffed into our mini-fridge, and I hope Mary Jo won't get mad at me for sabotaging her diet.

It is soooooooooo cold. Halloween, Wisconsin-style. You must sprint from house to house to collect hot chocolate instead of candy. Ended up working late (a few more weeks of this and I'll pay back the bank), then went to Halloween party in dorm. No costume for me. Everyone on floor yelling at me for not playing along. I'll probably start another faction war over this.

Mary Jo was in our room all night doing her best to avoid temptation of candy corn and candy in general. She looked completely miserable. Also a bit on the pale side.

"Have you been eating anything except that weird program food?" I asked her.

"No," she said. "And it's not weird!" She slammed down her chemistry book and grabbed the bottle of "Super Energetic Vitamin Boost" that goes with this diet, started shaking pills into her mouth with her shaky hand.

The woman is in desperate need of a good smoothie. She needs fruit and energy boosts. So do I.

7 P.M. At my Fun-Times Funders shift. Dying for it to be over so I can go home, write my poli sci paper. Just had very awkward conversation with WW III. He said, "So this weekend, I was thinking we could work on our next protest together. Maybe—"

"Actually, I can't," I said. "I'm going home."

"You are? All the way to Colorado? For a weekend?"

Felt my face turning red. "It's a long weekend. And it's, well, to see my boyfriend," I said. "He got me a ticket, and so . . . I'm going to visit him."

"Oh. I see." He went back to his cubicle.

Am I letting down the cause? But what about *my* cause: seeing Grant?

10:30 P.M. Here I am with 8 books, 3 legal pads, 4 pens, 43 index cards, 6 completely blank discs—like I'll need more than 1—and 1 computer, and . . . 1 very confused mind.

How am I ever going to finish my paper before I leave for the airport? Oh well. Where there's a will, there's a way.

Sure.

Thyme and I are in dorm lounge. Moved our computers down here.

4:27 A.M. Well, I made my point on the first page and it's followed by 6 pages of beating around the bush. Thyme's is the opposite.

173

Have to write 3 more pages to make it 10. Chugging iced tea. Trying to stay awake, but I think I got the caffeine-free kind by mistake.

6:24 A.M. Sunrise watching can be fun but in its appropriate time and place. Paper is almost finished. Thyme went to caf to get us donuts and coffee. Like we need coffee. Like we can even hold a cup.

7:30 A.M. Medical alert! I was staggering back to my room from the lounge, needing to print paper and get dressed for class. Mary Jo was walking toward me in robe and slippers. But she was weaving a little, as if following a line on the floor only she could see. Then she fainted! She totally keeled over! Her bucket dropped onto the carpet, and horsey shampoo and conditioner splattered on the walls. Waiting for Thyme to wake up Annemarie to borrow her car and then bring car around; taking MJ to campus health.

9:10 A.M. Have been waiting 2½ hours for someone to look at Mary Jo. Thyme left to go hand in our papers. Assistant gave Mary Jo a cursory glance and decided she was "non-emergencial," and promised to return. Have been up to the desk 6 times demanding help. Each time, Mary Jo tries to escape but is too weak, can't make it to the exit before I catch her.

Called her parents but got Ed instead. Told him that Mary Jo wasn't feeling well and it might be good if her family visited this weekend.

"Are *you* going to be there, Courtney?" Ed asked.

"No, that's why I thought you should come by," I said. "Because I have to go home to Denver for the weekend."

"Oh. Well, she'll probably be all right," Ed said. "Once she eats a decent meal."

So we're going to blow off the health center and go to Mary Jo's favorite breakfast place, Koffee Kitchen. My treat.

Same pen, different story.

I'm home! I can't believe it. I am actually about to go to sleep in my very own bed in my very own room with my very own psycho dog lying on the floor next to me.

Got in pretty late, so Grant and I could only hang out for an hour before Mom selfishly demanded he leave because it was after midnight. She said she wanted to talk to me. Our talk consisted of "What would you like for breakfast?" and "What are your plans?" and "Are you getting all A's or not?" But at least she did say she's definitely *not* seeing that chat room guy, or any other Internet guys.

Anyway, big news: Grant has a goatee now. Very weird when I saw him, but he does look even better than before. Typical Grant, he keeps it cut really short and neat. Discovered that I still love him to death even though he devoured the cheese basket I brought him within minutes, like a giant mouse, and didn't bring me anything.

Okay, so he bought the ticket. No problem there.

But not even 1 flower???

Mary Jo's stupid Joe even gave her bouquets. And isn't Grant a better person than that?

Okay. I am not going to spend the weekend thinking about that idiot Joe, or Mary Jo, or anything back at CF. Except maybe to hope that Mary Jo is eating real food.

I hate it here. I'm miserable. I wish I were in Wauzataukie.

Now that's a sentence I never thought I'd write.

Maybe I can catch an earlier flight back tomorrow. I could spend the weekend working on our ban-CFC act for next weekend. I am wasting my time here.

Can I really be saying this? Are things that bad? YES.

This was *supposed* to be a romantic trip. Grant and I were going to spend the weekend in each other's arms. We'd go to all our favorite places, cuddle, snuggle, etc.

So much for having a romantic weekend. I've ruined everything, or Grant's ruined everything, I don't know who's responsible. But tonight we got into the biggest fight we've ever had. (Maybe because we've never fought. Period.) It's because Grandmother Superior has bronchitis and sounds awful. Okay, I know that she has lived with Grant and his folks for the past couple of years since his grandfather died, and he's really close to her and she's really close to him, etc. But does she have to get bronchitis on the one weekend we can see each other?

So tonight he said he had to stay home and keep an eye on her because his parents had a business dinner thing. Hello! It's *Friday night*. I just got here last night, and this morning I had to hang out with my mom while he went to classes and then this afternoon he had to work for 4 hours, because he couldn't get anyone to cover that part of his shift.

So then he came down to meet me in Denver, and

what does he want us to do? Not go out here. Not go back to Fort Collins so we can hang out in his room and I can meet his roommate and his friends and go to a party there. No. He wants to sit around holding Grandmother Superior's hand! One of us on each side of her! It's *only* bronchitis, I told him. Even his grandmother told him not to be silly, that he should go out with me.

"You should," I said, trying to ignore her rattling cough. "I mean, Grant, you do see her all the time," I whispered.

"No, I don't," he said. "You don't know, Courtney. I haven't been down here at all lately. And she needs me, okay?" He really sort of snapped at me.

The unflappable Grant was actually very, very stressed out. It made me feel awful but I didn't know how to deal with him. So I came home. What else could I say? But now I feel worse.

Saturday afternoon, waiting for Grant to come over. Just had lunch with Beth. We spent like 3 hours going over everything and everyone new in our lives. I was afraid I was boring her with too many stories, but she was totally into it.

All in all, though, I didn't get a good feeling from her. I think she is failing out, though she didn't say that. And why aren't she and Bryan spending more time together?

I guess part of it is that I just can't help thinking that the only reason Bryan and Beth got together is because the dating pool at Bugling Elk had gotten a little shallow, esp. for Beth, who had a new fling every other weekend and had already dated a bunch of the seniors and juniors and had to seek out a sophomore. So I'm expecting her to want to break up with him, because she has a whole new pool of college guys.

Anyway, all through lunch, I couldn't stop staring at her hands. Her index finger was discolored. That's when I knew she was totally smoking again. "But it's different now. I'm only a social smoker," Beth said when I confronted her about it. "I only smoke at parties."

"You just told me that you go to parties almost every night! That means you're smoking *every day*."

"Oh," Beth said, like she hadn't realized that.

I grabbed her purse. She thought I was going for her smokes—which would have been easy, because there were like 2 or 3 packs inside—but I pulled out her wallet.

"Courtney, what are you doing? Stop that!" She lunged for the wallet.

Just as I suspected. Those charred-lung photos she used to carry around all the time to convince herself—and others—never to smoke again were gone. But why did she get so nervous when I picked up her wallet? "We used to share everything," I reminded her. "So why do you care if I look at your wallet?"

"It's private, that's all." She grabbed it back from me.

It took me all night to figure out why she didn't want me to look at her wallet. That's when I realized something I hadn't seen inside. Thyme's photographic memory must be growing on me. Bryan's picture wasn't in there anymore. And I can't stop thinking about what that means and what I'm supposed to say or do about it.

Oh well. At least things are good between me and Grant. I guess that sounds selfish, but last night turned out to be very romantic. Started out pathetic (see above) and I sat around being extremely unhappy for hours. No one else was home. Bryan was away for a cross-country meet and Mom was out with friends. It was me and Oscar. Together again. Not that I don't love him, but. So I decided there was only one way to repair the weekend. I took Oscar for a long walk. Thought this would create good karma for me, as spending quality time with pet with trauma-induced epilepsy only can.

Then the more I walked, the more I realized I wanted to make up with Grant—immediately. Actually half dragged Oscar all the way over to Grant's house.

While I was moping at home, Grant had gone to Safeway and bought cough drops for Grandmother Superior, flowers for me. When I got there we hugged for a really long time. He apologized for being selfish when it came to his grandmother. I apologized for being spoiled and unreasonable. But he said I wasn't unreasonable, the whole point of me coming to visit was for *us*.

I never realized that we hadn't actually had a fight before. I hated it, and don't want it to ever happen again. I was going to have us sign a pledge to that effect, but realized that would be childish and also like a prenuptial agreement or something.

So I just told him how I didn't want to leave on Sunday and how we only had 48 hours left.

"Then we'd better make the most of it," he said. So we went upstairs and did.

Hope Grandmother S. was really asleep, like Grant thought.

On plane now. Thyme and Annemarie will pick me up at airport. I should be studying but I'm not. I keep thinking about what a weird and good weekend it was.

Had wonderful Saturday night: Beth, Bryan, Grant, and I went out to dinner, then Grant and I hung out, then today we went to the zoo and walked around holding hands and being disgustingly romantic. At the airport when we were saying good-bye, I couldn't help crying, because I really didn't want to leave.

Grant gave me this gigantic Superior squeeze right before I was getting on the plane, when they started calling rows. "So what do you think of the goat? You never said." He took my hand and brushed his chin with my fingers.

"I like it," I told him. "What about my hair? *You* never said."

"Well, it shows off your gorgeous ears," he said.

Which is exactly what Mary Jo said! But then Grant started kissing my ears. So it wasn't really the same as Mary Jo saying it after all.

When I got on the plane, I was too flustered and in love to find my seat. Flight attendant asked if I was an unaccompanied minor. Very embarrassing.

Spent all morning lying in bed rehashing wonderful weekend with Grant. Then the day got worse all of a sudden.
Realized I was going to be late for work. Sprinted to get
ready. Still got there half an hour late and had to endure
lecture from Jennifer. Endless blather about how I was
letting down the New Product Team; never mind that the
products aren't *new* anymore.

Then tonight, Beth called. She and Bryan broke up!
"I can't believe you broke up with him," I said. Were they
waiting for me to leave town or something?

"I didn't," she said.

"Oh, you mean it just sort of happened—it was
mutual. Wow. You must be upset. I'm so sorry," I told her.

She muttered something about how they were holding it together for my visit but. . . . And then I couldn't
understand the next couple of sentences. She was crying
and smoking and crying and coughing.

"If you're that upset, maybe you guys shouldn't break
up," I told her. "Are you sure it wasn't just a big fight, and
you guys need to kiss and make up?"

"No . . . but . . . see . . . " And then the garbled gook
again.

It was breaking my heart to hear her cry like that.
"On the plus side?" I said. "It *was* the longest relationship
you've ever had."

She started crying even harder and then she had to
hang up. I don't know, I thought it was a valid point.

I waited a little while, then called Bryan. He seemed remarkably unfazed. "I really don't want to talk about it with you," he said.

"It's okay, B. You can open up to me. I won't tell her anything you say, I promise."

"I just don't want to go into it. You wouldn't get it, anyway." He's always saying that, like he's Einstein and is dealing with the mysteries of the universe, and I'm not. "I'm fine," he said. "I'm actually relieved. I'll have a lot more time for training now."

Typical Bryan. Acting like nothing's wrong when his whole world's crumbling. Well okay, not whole world. Just the girlfriend part of it.

Anyway, Bryan and Beth were going out before me and Grant. So the fact they broke up now means . . . nothing. It has nothing to do with us. NOT AN OMEN. They only live a few miles from each other, so if they couldn't make things work, then their relationship must have been doomed.

I am a little peeved at Beth, though. I have to admit. But since she's the one who's upset, and Bryan sounds okay, I guess I won't be mad at her. It had to happen sooner or later. Now they're both "free and clear." Wonder if they'll get back together. Wonder if Bryan will find someone at Bugling Elk. Wonder who Beth will hook up with first, and how long it will take her.

Must call Jane now to place my bet. I give Beth until . . . let's say Thanksgiving. I bet she'll hook up with someone before then.

Thyme and I got into a huge HUGE argument in the hall today. We were trying to make plans and signs and stuff for our big final protest on Saturday and we kept disagreeing about everything. All of a sudden she *totally* switched sides and said that changing the school's initials was a really thoughtless idea because it was history, and we'd be *contaminating* an historical site, including her father's—grandfather's—Econ building, etc.

So I demanded to know whether she came from money or not, because I saw her parents' Jag, and if they lost all their money then why didn't she have to work, and why would she lie about that, because I didn't care one way or the other. And she said, "*Obviously*." She said if I had any morals at all I'd never go serve meat and cheese at Bagle Finagle as a vegan, and I was probably not even a *real* vegan or even a vegetarian, which is *so* ridiculous! So then I told her that she obviously had a trust fund, which made it so stupid that she was running around preaching about only working PC jobs and she didn't have any life experience at all doing anything—

We were screaming at each other in the hallway. Really ridiculous. Mary Jo came out of our room and told us to break it up. We didn't, and were about to get into a cat fight when Mary Jo hauled me away like I was a stray cow. Slammed door behind us.

"Why do you even bother?" she asked me.

"What?" I asked.

"She was being so mean to you—I can't stand it!" Mary Jo said. "Do you know she was criticizing your idea the whole time you were gone?"

"Wh—what?" I said.

Mary Jo nodded. "She said it was stupid and counterproductive."

"Are you sure that's not what *you* think?" I asked.

Mary Jo shrugged. "Maybe I don't think your idea is great, but I don't *pretend* to support it while I go around telling everyone that it isn't. I'd never undermine you—or any friend—like that."

"So you don't think it's great," I said. "Well, I'm not surprised, but—"

"But I think the fact you're that passionate about it is awesome," Mary Jo said. "You obviously care a lot about this place."

What? I thought. What was she talking about? This protest isn't about making CFC a better place, it's about . . . well, anyway. Can't believe Thyme would desert me and our CFC protest now, after everything. Not a friend. But I didn't like hearing Mary Jo say it. I don't *have* any other friends here. Even though Thyme can be a jerk, what am I supposed to do? Toss her aside?

Mom called tonight when I got home from library, and she was so excited, it was great. She met some single guy at a banquet where Bryan was getting an award. His daughter's a cross-country star and so they really hit it off, because Bryan and his daughter also hit it off, so it was like stereo dating, they had tons to talk about, and well, did she mention he's handsome and a runner himself, etc., etc., blah blah blah.

"So did you ask him out?" I said.

"What? What do you mean? Of course not," she said.

"Mom!" She drives me crazy when she does this.

Peña was doing Tarot card readings in her room, so I grabbed a Fresca for her, went in, and asked her if she could give me some info on Mom. Like, will she ever date this guy?

The Fool card kept coming up. Not sure about that. I really don't want my mom getting involved with a jerk after all these years of celibacy. Peña kept saying the fool didn't mean an actual fool, but it did seem sort of coincidental. "Your luck is going to change soon, Courtney. That's what it means."

"For the better?" I asked. "Right?"

"Mm." She glanced up at the doorway. "Next?"

That doesn't seem good. Does it?

Called Grant to talk about the Bryan and Beth situation and my fight with Thyme and my big protest, which is only *2 days away*. But he wouldn't get into analyzing Beth and Bryan and wanted only to talk about Bugling Elk's Homecoming, which is this weekend. I felt like even though I was just there, all of a sudden we were living in parallel universes. Different worlds. Whatever. Him: stuck in Colorado, clinging to high school. Me: free-floating anxiety in Wisconsin. Living "so on the fringe."

"I can't believe you won't be here," Grant said. "It won't be the same without you."

"Make sure you say hi to everyone for me," I said. "And keep an eye on Beth. And take notes. I want to know how everyone's doing. And tell everyone I'm doing incredibly great here. You know. *Lie*."

Grant laughed. "You *are* doing great. Aren't you?"

"Sure," I said. "Actually, things are pretty good. I've got this huge thing happening on Saturday and—"

"Agh! Court, I hate to do this to you, but I've got another call," Grant said. "It's probably my lab partner, Melinda—I'm supposed to be meeting her to study for our exam tomorrow. Can I call you when I get to Denver?"

"Sure," I said, gulping for air. "Okay."

Lab partner Melinda??? Who is *that*? Why haven't I heard about her before? Suddenly very uneasy about everything.

OH MY GOD

Just got off the phone with everyone from home. *Everyone*. First the Tom called on his cell phone. The Tom! It was so fun to talk to him. Can't believe he's still at Bugling Elk, still working in Principal LeDuque's office to make up for money he embezzled last year. Still scoring with freshmen (fresh girls) even though he is now a Senior Plus. Disgusting pig. He totally made me laugh, though, because he kept describing everyone at the party and who had changed and who hadn't. And he said a million times how much he missed me.

Then he gave the phone to a bunch of other people who said hi, then Beth got on the phone. I kept teasing her about who she was going to pick up at the party, now that she was single again. Maybe the Tom? Who knows. Then she gave the phone to Grant. And it was just so cool to talk to him because I almost felt like I was there with him and everyone else.

I just love him and all those guys *so much*. I can't wait to see them!!!

Christmas seems like way too far away. I can't wait to see Grant, and Beth and even the Tom!

This is now the journal of Courtney Smith, Media Star.

This was me in front of TV camera today: "Yes, it was my idea."

This was the reporter (from world's smallest TV station, but who cares): "It's *very* innovative."

Watched her report tonight, and a lot of the coverage was actually about all the people who disagree with us. But this is just the beginning! Although I'm not sure how we'll get enough exposure now that football season is ending. Oh well. We'll think of something.

Final home game = biggest turnout yet.

We did our dramatic piece after Annemarie tapped into P.A. system, announced that the Not-Ready-to-Lose-the-Ozone-Layer Players would be performing "Why We Shouldn't Be Known as CFC."

(Okay, so we could have worked more on the title but we got all caught up in being psyched about our name.)

Half of us dressed in aerosol-can costumes made by these awesome new theater people. The other half of us were trees, the rain forest. A small rain forest, okay, but still legit. Cans ran around spraying the air wildly (with water); trees withered and died; lone iceberg in the show melted; Erik ran across field with his pale skin painted red, simulating intense sunburn due to no ozone protection.

Brilliant. Artistic. Some people laughed at us, but that was okay. Thyme even showed up at the last minute to portray a green shrub; we could hardly tell it was her. At first I was mad at her for being hypocritical, but then forgot and was so psyched about our performance that I hugged her once we got off field. We walked around in our wilting costumes, waving at the crowd whenever they cheered or jeered us. At one point Corny put his arm around me as we posed for the school newspaper photographer, and he pulled me really, really close, to where it was actually sort of embarrassing, but at the same time I sort of liked getting a bear hug from a cornstalk.

We all went out to celebrate tonight; spent hours and hours sitting in booths discussing philosophies of life, music, etc. We were having fun, and then we all got into a serious conversation about having divorced parents and reasons never to get married and how marriage was an overrated, outdated concept.

Gone all day. Got home and there were 5 messages: 3 from the Tom, 2 from Grant. What's up with the Tom? Did he get drunk and decide to hit on me after all these years?

Talked with the Tom this morning.

Not going home for Christmas.

Not going home ever again.

Beth and Grant. Tom said they were making out Friday night.

Complete, utter betrayal.

To hear it from the Tom, worst of all. Grant not home when I called (of course) so I got the Tom first.

So. That's why Beth and Grant both wanted to stay in Colorado for college. To be close to each other. Grant never got over their fling during junior year and has been pining for Beth ever since. Probably only dating me to kill time until Beth broke up with Bryan. God. I've been such a fool. It was so obvious.

So it all makes sense on some level. But logic doesn't mean I can stop crying. Why didn't I see this coming?

Hate them both.

Must call Jane now and tell her I lost the bet. Beth hooked up with someone before Thanksgiving. GRANT!

Will this day never end? Worst day of my life and it won't end.

Here is what Grant said. I think. I was so mad and hurt that my hearing was going in and out, like bad radio reception.

They were drunk at the Homecoming party. And after they called me, they drank more, and they kept talking about me, and how much they *missed* me and how *great* I was. And then they were drinking more punch. And Beth was talking about how much she missed Bryan, and . . .

Oh, ick. I can't continue to write this down in MY journal. It's so . . . I don't know. Humiliating? Tawdry?

Mary Jo keeps asking if I'm all right. We ran out of tissues about two hours ago and my face is getting raw from using cheap dorm TP to cry into. No, I'm not all right, isn't it obvious?

She went out and came back with a pack of Twizzlers from the vending machine in the basement. "I'll call my brothers and ask them to beat up Grant. Okay?"

"*No*," I said. "Just leave me alone!"

Like licorice and farmers could help me now. I don't *think* so.

LATER . . .

Grant just called again to try to explain what happened. Mary Jo, Thyme, and Annemarie, who've been huddling around me for the past hour, all left to give me some privacy.

Okay, so. Grant and Beth were at Homecoming. I wasn't.

"Yes, I know I wasn't there, but if you even attempt to say that this is somehow my fault—"

"Courtney, I didn't say anything like that," Grant said. "I wanted you to be there, and you weren't, but I understand."

"Well I don't," I said. "I really can't listen to this." I

hung up all of a sudden. Then I wished I hadn't, because I had to know the story and until I did, I was going to obsess endlessly. So I called him back and said "What?"

"Courtney, don't be so mad. Please, I can't stand hearing you so mad at me," Grant said. He started saying all these really sweet things and I started crying so then I had to hang up again. It's like I can only handle this 1 or 2 minutes at a time.

"So have you talked to Beth yet?" Grant asked the next time I called.

"No, and I don't plan on it," I said. "Why? Did you want to make sure your stories match up before you said anything to me?"

"There's no story!" Grant said. "Nothing happened, Courtney. Nothing serious. I mean, nothing at all. Not really."

How many times can you say "nothing" without having it become so incredibly obvious that it's SOMETHING?

"See, Beth and I—" he tried to say the next time.

"What? There's a you and Beth now?" Oh my God. I really needed some Pepcid AC if he was going to continue. A whole box of it. Maybe two.

"Courtney, come on. You *know* me. You know I'd never do anything—"

"Tom told me that you and Beth *made out* at a party, at Homecoming. You kissed her, you . . . " God. What had he done? Did I want to know? Wasn't it all over between us, anyway? If so, couldn't I hang up without hearing this?

So I did.

Grant called back. "Before you hang up, I just want to say that I'm not going to call you again tonight. But please, Court. You've got to forgive me! I . . . I'm so sorry, and it didn't mean anything to me. You're the one who matters, okay?"

I "matter?" What does that mean?

Hung up, opened door, let Thyme, Mary Jo, Annemarie back into room. I just want to wake up tomorrow and pretend today didn't happen.

6:15 A.M. Oh crap. Just woke up. It wasn't a dream.

8:00 P.M. Jane is here. She drove all the way from Madison and even skipped her classes today and is spending the night to help me deal with all this. (I called in sick to BF. Mark/Marc/Marque asked what was really wrong and I burst out crying, told him whole gory story.) Jane hasn't talked to Beth yet, but she said she doesn't believe anything serious really happened.

Over lunch, which I couldn't eat, I laid out the evidence. First you gather the evidence, then you prosecute. It was like being on *Law & Order*, except I was nowhere near as pretty as that woman lawyer with the dark brown hair, esp. with my growing-out crew cut. I had a feeling I needed her help on this case, but, oh well. I told Jane what I thought, and what I knew.

She nearly fell off her chair. "You know, maybe you're right," she said. "Not about any of that conspiracy theory stuff. But maybe they were still attracted to each other. Subliminally, you know."

"Jane!" I screamed. "Don't say that!" The woman is taking two psych classes and suddenly thinks she knows everything?

"But you said it," she reminded me. "And I think you're onto something. It doesn't mean that they actually *wanted* to betray you, but maybe they couldn't help themselves—"

I raised my eyebrow and glared at her. "Don't even start with that. They could have just, you know. Unlocked their lips and walked away." I dropped my head onto the table and started crying again.

"Courtney, it's going to be okay. You'll be fine. You're strong. And look—maybe we don't know the whole story. I bet there's something we don't know."

"Like how I'm supposed to get on with my life?" I asked.

"I'll talk to Beth about it," Jane said. "Let's not rush to judgment."

"Oh, yeah, let's not do that. Just because my boyfriend and my best friend slept together . . . I wouldn't want to *judge* them or anything."

"They didn't sleep together!" Jane said. "It was a kiss, only a kiss. It was probably only a peck on the cheek. And we're getting our information from the Tom, remember? He exaggerates *everything*. I mean, some girl smiles at him, and he'll go around telling everyone they did it in the computer lab." She smiled uneasily. That's what happened to her when she first came to Bugling Elk.

She tried to get me to calm down by taking me on a drive through the country, past many many cows, and buying me a cute little basket of apples and a caramel apple and some honey. Then she insisted on going into cutesy gift shops and buying me cutesy barrettes to clip my hair with. Actually looks sort of stylish now. But who cares? Not Grant. Not me.

This morning after Jane left, I packed a duffel and went to the motel where the Greyhound bus stops. I have like $40 to my name and was prepared to spend it all. Turned out there were about 4 hours until the next bus. The lady behind the desk looked like she was about to phone the authorities because I looked completely unbalanced. But I waited. I don't know where I thought I was going. Something vague involving Phoenix, going to my dad's. Not that he'd be much help. I didn't know where to go. I just didn't want to be stuck at CFC and I didn't want to be back home.

So I sat in this really lame waiting area and after an hour, the lady behind the desk came out and started telling me about the Runaway Hotline, and gave me a brochure on suicide prevention, and I realized I really did have to stop sobbing in public. Very embarrassing. Also realized that I was turning into my dog, Oscar. Bolting at first sign of trouble.

I poured my heart out to this lady over a cup of instant decaf. I told her how I loved Grant and how Beth knew that, and how just because she was upset about not dating my brother anymore, she didn't have to choose Grant to get over Bryan with, okay so maybe they did have a thing before he and I got involved, but that was just physical attraction, and since when was that more important than love?

"I hate to tell you, honey," she said. "But a lot of

times, it's *the* most important thing."

I asked for the suicide brochure back, and a refund on my ticket, and decided to walk back to campus.

The thing is that if I had a car, I'd be gone by now. That's probably why Mom wouldn't let me have the Taurus, she knew something like this would happen. She's never believed in relationships working out. Why didn't I listen to her? Never gave her credit for being brilliant.

Why didn't I listen to myself? I was not supposed to get involved with anyone. I *swore* I wouldn't. But no, Grant had to force himself into my life, even though I made it totally clear I was not interested in seeing anyone. Such a *Grant* thing to do. Pushy, insistent, rude.

My favorite person in the entire world.

Formerly known as Superior.

Now known as Inferior.

Yes, so, okay, things can get worse. Not much I guess, but still.

I went to work this afternoon, but only so I could try and sneak in some phone calls to Mom, Alison, and Jane. Had only gotten to Alison (who was being really sweet and supportive) when Dean S. materialized beside my cubicle. He was actually carrying one of those paddleball things and whacking the rubber ball on a string all over the place.

I hung up the phone and tried to smile at him. "Hi, Dean Sobranksy."

"Courtney," he said, the red ball flailing wildly close to my head. "Your event on Saturday was really out there."

At first I didn't even know what he was talking about. I had completely forgotten about the fact I had even done something *fun* on Saturday, before I found out that what's-his-name and what's-her-name had ruined my life.

Dean S. started on this extremely-polite-yet-still-a-rant about how he certainly appreciated the creative process more than anyone, and that perhaps I didn't know that he was the Dean of Arts & Sciences at the college where he used to work, before this position became open, but couldn't I see that my friends and I were ruining what was a really fine year for Cornwall Falls in terms of academic and athletic achievements and—

The whole time he was talking, I was getting more

and more choked up, because the last thing I needed was him yelling at me on top of everything else.

"I'm sorry!" I finally burst out. "But I'm not responsible for anything that happened last weekend!" Tears started streaming down my face. So embarrassing.

"But, uh, Courtney, you were there," Dean S. said. "You were dressed like a can of deodorant." Stopped playing with the stupid paddleball and started trying to edge away from my desk.

"I'm not talking about a protest, who cares about a dumb meaningless protest," I wailed, or something to that effect.

"Oh? Are you giving it up, then?" Dean S. started to get excited.

I shook my head as I mopped my eyes with Kleenex.

"But you might cut back. Is that what you're saying?" Dean S. asked hopefully.

"Can't you see that I'm upset?" I asked.

He didn't say anything for a minute. Then he asked if I heard about the weather front coming in—it might be very windy, so I should take care to bring an extra coat, did I have something that kept out the wind but also kept in the warmth, did I own any Gore-tex etc., etc., blah blah blah.

The fact that he refused to ask me what was wrong made me *want* to tell him more. The next thing I knew I was pouring out my heart to him, describing whole heinous scene of Grant cheating with Beth, Beth cheating with Grant, everyone cheating on Courtney.

Dean S. looked like he couldn't get out of there fast enough. So much for sympathy to student affairs. He didn't say one word in sympathy, or get me a new tissue when I soaked the last one on my desk.

But then he silently picked up all my assigned index cards for the day and distributed them to other people, and he said I could go home and asked if I wanted someone to go with me. Very nice offer, but I said no. Then, as I was leaving, I saw Wittenauer watching me. Gave him a pathetic little wave and ran out. Too embarrassing, because I would have told him everything, too, and don't enough people know already?

In retrospect: would I have wanted to hear Dean S.'s opinion? Probably not. He'd say something about how I was too "mat-oor" to be getting upset over a boy. I wish. Why must I always be getting so distraught over them, though? First Dave, now Grant. They end up stealing days, weeks of my life, because I become unable to do anything but mope and cry. Not worth it.

"Dear Courtney,
I know you'll want to delete this as soon as
you see who it's from. I don't know how I can
make it up to you. I should never have kissed
Grant, I should never have spent any time with
him that night, I was too on the edge because
of me and Bryan breaking up. So I made a
huge mistake. And now I've ruined the best
friendship I've ever had. It wasn't planned, and
it's not anything that would ever happen again.
We kissed, and that's it. Grant pushed me away
and said, "This is wrong!" He's a great guy, he
loves you so much. And I wish I'd never gone
to that party. Love, Beth"

Have to take down all the photos on my bulletin
board. Especially the ones with Beth and Grant in the
same shot. Have to take those outside and burn them in
the approved smoking area.

LATER ...

Not going to classes. Sitting in lounge watching
Montel. Today's topic is "Teen Girls Who Remind Me a
Lot of Beth." They're all backstabbing sluts who ruined
other people's lives, like for instance sleeping with best
friend's boyfriend.

Maybe I should write to Montel, see if I can get on

the show. Not that I've ever enjoyed having my dramas played out in public. I mean, I got plenty of that in high school.

Which reminds me. Does everyone at Bugling Elk know about the Grant and Beth fling? Of course they do. The Tom does not know the word "secret" or "discretion."

Here is us on *Montel*, here are our running blurbs:

"Courtney: Won't forgive her ex-best friend even if she begs."

"Beth: Begging for forgiveness."

"Courtney: Still saying no."

Then Grant would come out after listening backstage and the audience would boo him. And he'd look shocked because he hasn't been booed in his entire life. (Except for when he was short and skinny when young and got picked on, but that's jeering, not booing. Anyway this is a fantasy, so who cares.)

Grant would probably wear the shirt I gave him for his birthday. He's *that cruel*.

Montel would hold my hand while I sobbed and spat out the details. One problem with this: I don't know the details. And I can't know them. Ever.

Ben and Marque—no, wait. New name tag today. Now Marcus. Jennifer is furious because he's using up all the label-maker tape. Maybe I'll change my name, too. What variations are there on Courtney? Court . . . not? Cortland—like the apple?

Anyway, Ben and Marcus insisted we go straight to a party from work, as I was being far too much of a downer. Marcus doing everything possible to make me laugh. Kept grabbing customer comment cards and writing comments about the customers on them, like: "Your shirt and those pants? I don't think so."

"You know what would really cheer you up? A malt," Marcus said.

"It's like ten degrees out," I said.

"Yeah. Like that matters. I'll be right back."

"If you think about the temperature here, you'd never go out and do anything," Ben told me while he was gone. "Don't worry, you'll adjust."

Can I just say that I'm really tired of trying to adapt and adjust?

Marcus came flying through doors five minutes later with 3 giant cups from Koffee Kitchen, one for each of us. "Oh, wait—you're not supposed to have milk, are you?" he said as he handed mine over.

"Give me a straw," I said. "Now."

"Ooh, she's living on the edge," Ben said. "I've heard

of drowning your sorrows before, but did they mean in frozen custard?"

"Technically, for her, this is worse than getting drunk, because she's cheating on her diet."

"It's not a diet!" I said, laughing. "I just don't eat dairy." I looked down at towering whipped cream sculpture atop chocolate shake. "That, um, often."

"Uh oh. Brain freeze," Marcus said when he finished his in record time.

"I've had a brain freeze for the past two weeks," Ben said. "I got a seventy-two on my last econ test because I forgot to study an entire section of my notes. Now my average is an eighty-eight, and I have to pull it back up to an A."

"I don't think I'm getting any A's," Marcus said.

We were talking about our classes so intensely that we didn't even notice some customers had come in and were waiting for service until one of them rang the bagel-shaped bell on the counter. Nearly gave me a heart attack.

After we closed up, I went home, where I received the second biggest shock of my life. 2nd only to Grant/Beth Shocker.

Joe is back. In Mary Jo's life. In my life. In our *room*. Help me.

"So, you and that guy broke up?" he asked. "How come?"

Mary Jo hit him on the arm. "It's personal."

"Oh. He dumped you, huh?" He got this stupid smile on his face. "That blows."

206

"Gee, that means a lot to me, Joe," I said. "And he didn't break up with me."

"He could have at least waited until Christmas break and done it in person," Joe said to Mary Jo, like they were having a conversation and I wasn't in the room.

Am going to kill Mary Jo tomorrow.

Went to work this morning. Afterward, came to library, like other unattached people do on Saturdays, especially when they don't want to be in their rooms. Supposed to be studying for sociology exam now. Students of the World, Unite!

Here are the key terms: Capitalism. Historical (Hysterical) materialism. Bourgeoisie. Exploitation. Alienation. Proletariat. Etc., etc., blah blah blah, *revolt*.

Forget Marx. There is a little-known piece of literature, soon to become famous, known as . . .

The Courtney Manifesto

1. A specter is haunting Wisconsin. Her name is Beth. Or maybe his name is Grant. It's hard to actually see a specter.

2. I must figure out how to react as a reactionary. What does that mean, anyway?

3. I must free myself by stopping harmful, low-self-esteem thoughts from entering brain.

4. There is strength in numbers, so . . . bring 5 fingers together to make a fist.

5. Use fist to punch specter(s) in the nose, mouth, anywhere painful.

6. Don't forgive specters. Never listen to anything they say again.

7. Become dedicated to the cause. Any cause, so long as it does not involve people in Colorado.

8. Think only lofty thoughts regarding future of society, not future of my pathetic little life.

Manifesto is impossible to live up to. I can't stop obsessing about what was happening 1 week ago today. Tonight. I keep picturing Grant and Beth. I don't care if it only lasted 5 seconds, like they said. 5 seconds is too long.

Everything is so impossible to deal with, especially long distance. Oh God. Dave, such a Dave . . . I totally underestimated him. He was right. This is why he broke up with me last year. This is why LDRs don't work, whether they're half an hour away, half a country away. I can see it all so clearly now. That weekend I went home? It had already started. That's why Grant and I had such a hard weekend. He was probably only hanging out with his grandmother because he didn't want to tell me he'd rather be with Beth. Grandmother Superior was faking her illness, in on the plot. All a giant conspiracy. It started back when we applied to colleges. The reason Beth & Grant didn't protest my going so far away was because they already KNEW they wanted to hook up. It was all a conspiracy to get me out of state of Colorado.

First Beth was going out with my brother. Then she's going out with my boyfriend? What kind of a best friend is she? Regret telling her anything.

So maybe Thyme can be annoying as hell sometimes. But at least she's a moral person. And at least she's *there* for me.

Just went to library pay phone to call Thyme. She said she didn't have time to talk to me because she and Kirsten were going shopping at outlet mall. She also said that it was time for me to get over what happened and get on with my life.

What? Shopping with Kirsten? Has she lost her mind?

It's a sad day when Joe is actually looking like a better guy than Grant. Joe went to the cafeteria for brunch and brought back donuts and fresh fruit for me. Totally not like him. He's trying to win me over or something—maybe he realizes I'm not on his side and never have been, and suddenly it matters to him that I like him?

Or no. Probably just overestimated how much food he wanted and had leftovers.

Anyway, Grant called again this morning. We talked but it was completely awkward. He kept asking what I was doing for Thanksgiving, and if I was still meeting my family in Nebraska. I said no. I said I had to stay here and work, which isn't true, but I didn't want to tell him what I'm really doing—staying in the dorm with foreign students and other jilted students like self. Kept it vague.

It's snowing now. Hall is going sledding. Annemarie is threatening to drag me out the door in my pajamas, so I'd better get dressed.

LATER...

Got home and there was a message from Erik: "Courtney, where are you? We're ready to organize Phase Two but we need your help." Forgot all about Badicals meeting.

All for now. Hands are frostbitten and it hurts to write.

Life going downhill fast. I just looked up "finagle" in dictionary. It means "to obtain by trickery; swindle."

Stupid corporate office thinks it means some sort of hilarious caper or something. All those cute things about finagling. So stupid! How dumb of them to not even know they're blatantly advertising the fact that they *rip people off*.

There's this "regular" who comes in on Mondays. He always tries to flirt with me a little, and I always ignore it. But today—I just couldn't take it when he said, "Those new cranberry bagels look as sweet and delicious as you, Courtney." Stupid Thanksgiving theme. I mean is that rude and over-the-top or what???

"Actually they're really quite sour," I said. Like my mood. "Cranberries. They're like lemons."

That didn't even faze him. "You mean it makes your lips pucker? Now that I'd like to see."

Har har har.

So I made his bagel haphazardly (he orders *double* cream cheese so I gave him like a half ounce of cranberry walnut and that was *it*), didn't cut it in half neatly, didn't even clean the old chive cream cheese off the knife first, and didn't offer him a steal deal. He got his revenge by grabbing a customer comment card and covering it with comments while he ate his bagel, which couldn't have been so terrible, because he *did* finish it, and all he had to do was *ask* for more cream cheese on the side if he was so unhappy.

These customer comment cards are *so* stupid, and I'm not just saying that because I got all bad comments from this guy. "How was your visit?" Like it's a national *park* or something.

He kept glancing over at me while he was writing, like maybe he was sketching my portrait: *Still Life with Bagel Slicer*. Then he got up to leave and stuffed the comment card in the box. "Have a nice day, Courtney," he said. How *rude*.

I knew I had to get that card out right away. I ran around the counter and tried to pry it out, using the hot-bagel tongs. It took me a minute, tops. I really should have just put it in my pocket. But I had to see what the guy wrote.

Turned out that he filled both sides of the card with his insane ravings about poor customer service, plus he spelled my name wrong, plus he spelled "inconsiderate" wrong, plus I think he meant to say "snobby" instead of "snotty," plus his handwriting is really bad. I had just torn the card in half when Jennifer appeared. She grabbed both halves, read them, then asked me to come to her office, where she told me I was on BF "probation." "And what does that mean?" I asked.

"One more strike and you're out," she said.

"But that would only be a total of two strikes," I pointed out.

"Courtney, do you *really* want to have this conversation?" she asked.

Um, no.

"You know I value all your hard work. You know I trust you," she said. "But if you're going to be rude to the customers just because you don't like cranberries—"

"I love cranberries," I said. It's people I can't stand. Do I even want to keep working at a place that uses "probation"?

"All we have to do is write a bunch of really positive customer cards for you," Marcus said afterward. "To offset the negative press."

"Jennifer will never go for that," Ben said. "You just have to sort of fade into the background for a while. Thanksgiving break is coming, the place is closed because no one will be around, so she'll forget all about it."

"And think of it this way. You're on probation, so you should wear these!" Marcus reached for the handcuffs dangling down over the cash register. "You're going to look *so* tough and dangerous. You'll get a new boyfriend in, like, days."

"I don't want a new boyfriend," I said.

"Oh." Mark and Ben looked at each other.

"I mean, I'm still with Grant. Sort of," I said.

"Oh?" They nodded. "Well, okay."

"What?" I asked.

"Nothing."

"Nothing."

I hate how everyone keeps saying that. I also hate the idea of being on my "best behavior" from now on. What if my standard is too low?

Went bowling with Wittenauer and the two Joes tonight. "The miracle isn't that we're bowling," he said. "The miracle is that you've lived in Wisconsin for three months and you *haven't* been bowling."

Wittenauer thinks he's so much better than me because he is a) a junior, and b) a decent bowler.

Anyway, I was really surprised when he came by my dorm room. Unheard of. I assumed he wanted to discuss our next meeting/protest, since I'd blown off the last one. I thought it was cool he came over, but at the same time I felt so weird about going out with him alone. Doesn't he know I travel in a pack? "Let's ask Thyme!" I said, and knocked on her door before Wittenauer could protest.

"*Bowling?* God, no," she said. "Anyway, I'm packing." Acting like a real snob all of a sudden.

Then I heard Mary Jo getting home so I ran back across the hall and mentioned it to her. Unfortunately Joe was in the room at the time, so it ended up: me, Mary Jo, Joe, Wittenauer heading off to Badger Lanes. All together now: why is Joe still in Mary Jo's life??? Topic for a much longer entry.

Badger Lanes: very smoky place with many neon beer signs and seriously overworn shoes. They were having a Turkey Special: for every game you bowled, you got one free (a game, not a turkey). So we played enough games to give me carpal thumb syndrome.

A very distressing thing happened when we were

getting to our lane. We were sitting down to put on shoes and were entering goofy names on computer score thing, when somehow my Grant story came up. Okay, it was my fault. I mentioned that the last time I went bowling was after graduation with, uh, my, uh, boy, uh. Anyway.

"Dean Sobransky told me you and your boyfriend broke up," Wittenauer said as we were lacing up. "Sorry about that."

"Oh well." Felt my face get red. Then more red. Was probably blending in with hair color. "We didn't exactly break up."

"Did too," Joe said. "She doesn't even talk to him and she took down all his pictures and—"

"*Joe*," Mary Jo said sternly. "It's none of our business."

Yes, I agree.

Mary Jo kindly changed the subject to a discussion of her best game ever, how she and her brothers had their own team, how they taught her everything she knows, etc. Cast her a very grateful look as I shuffled up to select a giant pink ball.

Then Joe got all competitive with Wittenauer and they were arguing about rules. Mary Jo and I were sitting there awkwardly; felt like it was a double date that had gone terribly awry; but it was not a double date, it was just a very bad combination of people.

Also, Mary Jo can make even bowling shoes look cute. How can she get away with this? Tiny little 6 on the back of her shoes. Me? 9. Isn't there another way to keep track of shoes besides displaying the size? Not necessary on any *other* kind of shoe.

As I was bowling, I started to get a weird feeling (in addition to my sprained thumb). Started asking myself why Wittenauer wanted to take me out bowling. Has nothing to do with, like, anything we usually do. He asked what I was doing for Thanksgiving and I said nothing. I said I planned to just sort of hibernate in the dorm and I was looking forward to time alone in my room without anyone else around. Unfortunately I was saying that when Mary Jo came back from picking up a spare. She wouldn't sit next to me at the scoring table and insisted on sitting on Joe's lap instead. She knows exactly what will get to me and does it anyway. She is even bringing Joe to her house for Thanksgiving, not realizing that he doesn't deserve it, and that he will be beaten to a pulp by her brothers. Or maybe they're too nice for that.

Anyway, afterward, it was really, really cold out, but Wittenauer and I stood outside the dorm and talked anyway. Then I was about to go in when Wittenauer sort of jogged after me and tugged on my jacket sleeve and asked if I wanted to go out again sometime. To do something other than in an organized group, or at work. "It would be like a very small, exclusive group," he said cutely. "No roommate, no Joe. Two of us."

"I can't. I mean, I'm, uh, still seeing Grant, you know," I said.

"Oh," he said. "I didn't know. I thought . . . Sorry."

"It's okay. I mean, I'm sorry," I said. Totally awkward.

217

"Hey, no big deal. I just thought . . . So, okay, well, good night."

Parted on really uncomfortable terms. I'm glad we won't be seeing each other for a few days.

2 P.M. Mary Jo just left. Joe went with her. Everyone gone. Dorm deserted. Krystyne just came by, doing her "clear-out" check, told me I was supposed to be gone. This dorm isn't heated during break, so I have to move into another one. What?

A person pays a price for solitude.

Maybe this wasn't such a good idea.

Is it too late to hitch to Nebraska to meet family like original plan? Maybe I'll call that motel/bus station, check schedules.

2:35 P.M. "Well, hello, *you*," woman at motel/bus station desk said. "How are things going, honey? I'm so glad you called to catch up."

"Actually I was hoping to get to Ogallala, Nebraska," I said.

She checked everything on the computer, and then came back and said she had some bad news and hoped it wouldn't plunge me into another dark depression. I had missed today's last bus. No bus tomorrow due to Thanksgiving. I could leave Friday, but wouldn't get there until Saturday. Etc.

"Sorry, sweetie. Why don't you come to my house for Thanksgiving?" She invited me for like ten minutes straight, I said no for nine minutes straight, and then finally the conversation was over. She made me write down her address just in case. I will now put it on now-vacant bulletin board. You never know when you might need a friend. With, um, bus schedules at the ready.

9 P.M. You won't believe where I am right now. Sitting in a farmhouse bed under a giant down comforter, cup of hot herbal tea on bedside table. Heaven.

Mary Jo came back for me!!! She and Joe and parents got halfway to her house, and then she made everyone turn around and come back for me. There wasn't going to be enough room in the crew cab pickup, so they dropped off Joe at a convenience store sort of near his parents' house and came back for *me*. She marched upstairs and said, "Look, Courtney, I don't even know why I'm asking you this, because you've done everything in the world *not* to be my friend. But would you please come home with me for Thanksgiving? Because I don't want to leave you here alone, I'm worried about you, and I think it would do you a lot of good to just get out of town for a few days."

It was quite the speech, and I was very touched. She chose *me* over Joe? I quickly packed a bag, grabbed my backpack full of homework, ran downstairs to the idling car. Mr. and Mrs. Johannsen are shy but so sweet. At their house, they have a sign out front with their names and all the boys' names on it. Can't tell all the brothers apart yet (except for my pal Ed). Too many twins spoil the pot. Also, one of them hasn't spoken yet and I can't remember his name. Very strange, because Mary Jo doesn't look

220

anything like her brothers. They are very tall and strong and sort of thick-looking.

Mary Jo gave me a tour of the farm and told me about all the different kinds of cows you can have. Her family has Brown Swiss ones. They have really pretty coats, actually beautiful—color like elk antler velvet, sort of.

"I just can't thank you enough for taking me in," I said to the family as we were gathered in front of a giant ham carcass. Words did not fit picture.

"God, Courtney. You make it sound like you're an orphaned pioneer or something," Mary Jo teased me. Hearty laughter from six boys almost put out the two tall pumpkin-scented candles on the table. "This isn't *Little House on the Prairie*."

"It isn't?" I asked. Then I started to laugh uncontrollably, too.

Orphaned Pioneer. That's how I felt, okay?

Is it because for once in the past 5 years I'm not in charge of "all the breads" and don't have Grandpa hovering constantly at my elbow with a carving knife and a 25-pound turkey on a platter?

First off, this family does not even take off Turkey Day. I have never seen 8 people work so hard in my life. They are like this well-trained army of specialists. Milk division. They could start a dairy college and call it Milk U. Except that sounds vaguely obscene.

But what was so great was that they didn't *care* if I ate the turkey or not. I mean, they kept offering, like 10 times, and I kept saying, "No thank you," and that was just fine with them. Got the feeling they just enjoyed offering things again and again—ritualistic behavior that was part of the meal whether you ate turkey or not.

The mashed potatoes were completely lumpy and dreamy. They had a glass dish they called the relish tray, which wasn't filled with relish but with pickles and olives. When I ate everything on it, it miraculously got refilled, though I never saw it happen. Mrs. Johannsen made a green bean/onion-thingy casserole; MJ made fresh rolls; together they made 3 pies, all while I was still asleep. Only strange thing was the trademark red wobbly Jell-O sculpture, which I remembered from the day we met.

I love Mary Jo's family. They let me sleep until 10, they let me disappear into my room for hours whenever I want to, and don't get upset by it. Love it here.

Wonder how Grant is spending Thanksgiving. Wonder if he's having a good time. Probably watching endless football games with his dad. Probably not even missing me. He's home in Denver, and so is Beth. Best not to think about this, but to concentrate on positives in life. Like the fact there is leftover pie.

Just had the most incredible conversation with Mary Jo over breakfast!!! French toast. Yum. Forgot it was made with eggs and milk until 2 slices down the hatch. We were drinking the entire percolator of coffee, and conversation was flying. Mary Jo explained why she was back with Joe, even though she had ditched him for me for Thanksgiving; they'd already talked on the phone a couple of times. Which reminds me, I need to call Mom and tell her where I am so she doesn't worry. Anyway, Mary Jo was defending Joe.

"He's not that bad," she said. "He was really stressed about passing bio, and he still is. So he took it out on me. He apologized. Look, *we're* not the same, Courtney. So we're not going to like the same kind of *guy*."

Big relief. Because I thought she did like the same kind of guy—no—the same GUY, Grant.

So she told me how Joe never stopped saying nice stuff about her body now, and how stupid her extreme diet was, and how since she'd gone off it, she's been not even caring about weight anymore, which is the only way to be, I think. Of course I'm lucky in that, and probably shouldn't even talk about it, I said, because everyone in my family's sort of skinny. So then Mary Jo said, "My birth mother is really thin, you know. So I've got genetics on my side, too."

"Wait—your birth mother?" She has a birth mother? I mean, so do I, but—this was different.

"I told you I was adopted," she said. "Remember?"

She did? Gulp. Totally slipped my mind. I did remember her saying in our housing workshop that I never listened. This was really bad. "Oh, sure. And um . . . what about your brothers?"

"They're not. See, my mom really desperately wanted a girl, but she couldn't have any more kids after she had my youngest brother. So they adopted me."

"Right." I nodded. Had she told me that? And if so, when? "So um, do you know your birth mother? Or is this from pictures you've seen, or like . . . " LIKE WHAT, COURTNEY? I felt so clumsy and awkward with my lame questions, like I was drowning in quicksand and swallowing it at the same time. I suck. Haven't I listened to a word she's said? Well, no, not really. I've been sharing a room with her for almost 3 months and I don't know she's adopted? I *really* suck.

"Of course I know her," Mary Jo said. "She works at the town post office. We'll go down after lunch and I'll introduce you."

"That is so cool," I said. "I can't wait to meet her. I already love your whole family, you know, so I'm sure I'll like her." Pouring it on a bit thick, like the real maple syrup I was drowning my French toast in, because of a) sugar overdose, and b) guilt.

LATER . . .

Snowing. Blizzarding. Trip to post office was called off. Everyone sitting around eating cold turkey leftovers.

225

Mary Jo mentioned we could snowshoe to P.O., but then we realized her bio mom probably wouldn't be there by the time we got there. Ed said he could hook up horse and sleigh, which sounded awesome to me, but MJ said it was snowing too hard and we'd get stranded.

Instead sat around inside, first doing homework by the fireplace (a/k/a "napping"), and then watching TV. Very weird experience to watch *Sally Jesse* with 6 men looking over your shoulder. But I couldn't look away. The topic was Betrayal. The topic was Courtney's Life.

They were talking to girls whose former best friends had ruined their lives, while the "friends" waited in a secluded area. All of the guests reminded me of myself: and why is this topic on talk shows every time I watch them? Is it that common? And if so, what is the point of trying to find a new best friend?

The guest who was me kept describing everything that had happened to me. Little taglines floated at the bottom of the screen saying things like

Hates her best friend for stealing her boyfriend.
Says her best friend betrayed her and she'll never trust her again.
Says she doesn't want to be friends anymore.
Won't accept former friend's apology.
Can't stop reliving pain of phone call from the Tom.
Is sitting in a farmhouse for Thanksgiving because she can't face her family.

Once I started down this path, I had to run out of the room because I was crying. Ed and Mary Jo came after me and took me out to the barn and showed me how to milk a cow. Found myself thinking that cows are cute, if large. Felt like a hypocrite as I enjoyed entire, bizarre process. Except that I really only brought one pair of boots, so they're outside in the snow now because they got too smelly.

Met Mary Jo's bio mom today. Her name's Patty, and she gave Mary Jo a big hug and told her how beautiful she was. They seemed really close and I thought it was amazing, considering the circumstances. I noticed she had tiny feet like Mary Jo and same hair also.

"Well, she *was* thin," Mary Jo said as we left the post office, which was actually a sort of desk thing inside the Stop 'n' Go. "Ever since she gave up her walking route and started sitting behind the desk, she's gained weight." Mary Jo let out a long sigh that was a white puff in the sub-zero air. It reminded me of when Beth used to smoke when we walked to school in the winter.

"Mary Jo?" I said. "No offense, but you have to stop looking at everything and everyone based on pounds. Okay? Because you look fine, you're doing great at school, and nobody really cares. Okay?"

She explained how she never thought about it at all, really—not until she came to CF. She grew up with all those brothers, and everyone always told her she was pretty, and she never really compared herself to her high-school friends. Then she got to CF and felt totally overwhelmed, and she was living with me, the health nut. And Joe told her she was too big, and it just pushed all the wrong buttons. I always forget that other people have buttons, too.

"So I'll try to change," she said. "I'm sure it's really annoying, listening to me obsess about it."

"No, it's not that," I said. "It's just . . . I hate worrying about how I look, and I hate when my friends worry about it even more. Because there's more to life. And anyway, you know what? Screw genetics," I said. "My mom likes everything I don't. And this hair color? It's like, where did that come from? Nobody else in my family is a redhead."

"Um . . . well, your cut's sort of starting to grow in nicely," Mary Jo said.

We went home and had lunch. Mary Jo showed me her wall of ribbons in the den, all for raising and showing sheep at fairs. Then she told me that when she was little and got lonely for not having a sister, she went out into the barn and slept next to a goat. "You're the first roommate I've had since Chipper," she said. Then she realized how dopey she sounded and we laughed so hard it was sort of embarrassing.

Mary Jo went to help with some chore, so I went inside and sat down next to Mr. Johannsen at the kitchen table. Brother who refuses to speak came in, nodded awkwardly at me, grabbed a sandwich and ran out of the kitchen.

I was trying to be polite, so I asked Mr. Johannsen about what it's like to have his own business and whether he knew about that bovine hormone.

He started telling me all about how factory farms are taking over; how thousands of family farms have closed or gone out of business in the last 30 years. He told me about how hard it is to make a living. (Man was just looking for an opening, apparently.) He told me about a famous historical milk strike, where farmers dumped out all their milk to protest the low prices, and how they were planning another one soon. Didn't have the heart to tell him that I've been on my own milk strike for years. I started feeling really guilty. Maybe people like me are the reason family farms are going under. I had him pour me 2 glasses of fresh whole milk and drank them right away.

Now Mr. Johannsen thinks I am a "great gal," and Ed is even more in love with me because I hit it off with his dad.

I, however, have stomach cramps.

Got back to campus tonight. I can't believe it. Grant was here while I was gone. He *drove* the whole way, hung out for 2 days waiting for me, and then left.

There are 7 increasingly despondent messages from Grant on the answering machine, and he left this very very sweet letter for me:

Dear Courtney,

I don't know where you are, and it's killing me. How can you not be here? I risked speeding tickets, I risked getting stuck in snow drifts, and I risked sleeping in the hallway of this dorm of yours that apparently has no heat.

[Good thing Grant keeps that sleeping bag in the car, the one with a tiger print on the inside that I'm always making fun of because he's had it since 4th grade? Or 6th grade, as he claims.]

This campus is deserted and the whole town is sort of shut down. I looked for you at Bagle Finagle, but it was closed. Ended up having a turkey dinner at some place called Brat Wurstenburger, which I think you told me about once. The very nice people there all thought I was left on campus by myself for Thanksgiving and insisted on buying me dinner.

This campus (not including unheated Rankin Hall),

despite 3-foot-high snowbanks, is pretty nice, actually—small, but old, nice brick buildings, lots of history, lots of trees. But with you not being here the place seems like a dump. Where are you? I finally tracked down your mom and Bryan in Nebraska. She said you went to a friend's at the last minute, but she couldn't remember which friend's. I didn't know if that was true, or if she was just mad at me, which is entirely possible. But you're obviously not here, and I've already filled up the memo board on your door, not to mention your answering machine tape, so . . .

So I'm left here sitting in the freezing cold hallway, with my Discman on, listening to the CD you made me, wondering: where are you? Why aren't you here? I missed you like crazy before. Now that I'm here, where you usually are—where you live and sleep every single day—I miss you even more. I've got 100 things to say to you. I want to make things right between us. I love you.

And I guess I have to leave today if I want to get back to CSU for classes Monday, which I have to do. I'm sorry. I'm sorry I missed you. It would have been great. Next time I'll call first, and next time you'd better be here. Please call me as soon as you're back so I know you're okay.

Love,
Grant

Read letter and collapsed on bed, woozy from emotion. Mrs. Johannsen ran to get me a cold washcloth from the bathroom, and Mary Jo fanned me with her bio textbook. "I'm okay!" I said. "Really." It's just that I forgot how great Grant could be. I'd been trying to forget. And remembering all of a sudden was a complete shock.

Mary Jo keeps pacing around the room, telling me I'm crazy if I don't call Grant this second, if I don't get back together with Grant immediately. Look at all he did, read that letter again, listen to all those sweet messages!

"Do you have any idea how much that means? What he did? Driving out here when he only has a four-day break, and I'll bet he had to take time off from work, and do you have any idea how much homework someone in his program would have over Thanksgiving break? And he risked it all to come see you, and then sat here in town and worried about you for two days straight and—"

"Okay, okay! I'll *call* him," I said. "Tomorrow."

Can't sleep. Very excited about the Grant letter. Very, very, very excited.

7:30 A.M. Just called Grant. Woke him and roommate Matt up. Told him how sorry I was that I left town without telling him where I was, told him about my trip with Mary Jo and what a good time I had. Told him I loved his letter. He sounded groggy but happy. Still tired from the drive.

All I kept telling myself while he talked was "Grant doesn't know how to lie." So he must be telling the truth when he says nothing really happened that night except a really dumb kiss. But no matter how many times he says it, I still have my doubts. And it's like, how am I supposed to trust them when they are living within an hour of each other, and I'm on the other side of Nebraska, and then some? But then Grant drove out here. So that means something. Maybe it means that he is extremely guilty. But no. Just looked at letter again. Seems to be an act of love.

Oh crap. Have to run—late for work now, and I'm still on probation.

10:45 P.M. When I got to work, Jennifer was standing by the door waiting for me. "Remember what I said? One more strike and you're out?"

"So how was your Thanksgiving?" I asked as I took off my coat, scarf, hat.

"Oh, uh, fine," she said.

Totally threw her off by being exceedingly polite.

Trying to act like Mary Jo and her mom. I gave her a big smile, hugged Marcus, hugged Ben, put on my apron and immediately got to work.

"Three strikes?" Marcus said under his breath as we restocked cheese bins. "What does she think this is? Jail?"

"Isn't it?" I said, laughing.

"No, this is one of those hospitals for the criminally insane," Ben said.

Then funniest thing to date happened. Thyme came in. But I didn't even know it was her. She was waiting in line with her sister, both wearing lots of makeup, leather coats, skirts, leather boots, leather everywhere. But I honestly didn't recognize her until Ben said, "So Thyme. How was Chicago—uh, I mean Sheboygan?"

"Hello, Benjamin," she said. "Hello, Courtney. Mark." No emotion registering on her face. She had lipstick on. She had a purse dangling from gold chain with a cell phone hanging off it. Disgusting.

"Thyme?" I said. "Oh my God, how are you?"

More like: oh my God, WHO are you?

"Morgan, are you getting anything to drink besides a triple cap?" Her sister was down by the cash register, flashing a fresh 20, or maybe it was a 50. Tricia was making coffee drinks and chatting about the latest weather front with her.

"Would you grab an OJ for me, Thornton?" Thyme replied.

I was standing there thinking: Morgan? Thornton? What the hell? Thyme's ordering coffee drinks and a bagel with cinnamon cream cheese? I was unable to even speak.

"Did you guys hit the Anne Klein outlet yesterday?" Marcus asked as he prepared her bagel. "Or wait, maybe you have more of an Ann Taylor look going. Well, some Ann anyway."

"I was thinking Donna," Ben said as he looked at Thyme with this expression of complete disbelief.

"DKNY?" I said.

"More like DKWI," Ben said. I was starting to laugh.

"Or how about DWI," Marcus said. "Dressing while impaired."

Thyme narrowed her eyes at us. "Nice aprons."

Ooh! Cruel!

"*Morgan.* Your triple cap is getting cold," her sister said from a table by the window.

"Coming, Thornton! Talk to you guys later!" Thyme called over her shoulder.

Marcus, Ben, and I left standing there, stunned. Even Tricia came over and joined us.

"I *told* you she was a complete phony," Ben muttered.

"Does this mean she's going to shave now?" Tricia asked. "Because I really wish she would."

Then Jennifer came out, caught us all "clumping," and reminded us of company policy: only the batter is allowed to clump at Bagle Finagle!

I've got like 17 strikes now, but she is still allowing me to play.

Oh joy.

236

I heard Thyme saying good-bye to her sister this morning, so I immediately went across the hall to get the
scoop. "So Thornton's gone, now. You can go back to
being yourself," I said.

No response.

"Did your parents make you act like the way they
wanted you to?" I went on. "Because I know how hard
that can be."

Thyme just shrugged and gave me a bright smile.
"This is me, Courtney. I don't know what you're trying to
say."

I just stared at her long enough so that she did. "You
used to lecture me about not staying true to 'the cause,'"
I said. "You got mad at me for serving cream cheese."

"I was confused," Thyme said. "Anyway, I don't know
who you're trying to be, but I'm embracing my roots. Did
you see my new Honda yet?" Okay, that's not *exactly*
what she said, but that was the gist of it. Apparently she
had a breakthrough with her parents and has now
decided to accept who she is, blah blah blah. I think it's
more a case of: parents threatening to cut her off unless
she toed their line. It's very disgusting. Instead of Zen
Buddhist quotes, she now sounds like she's spouting lines
from mugs with smiley faces. What happened to former
best friend here? It's like she joined a cult. The cult of
Economic Inevitability. I *knew* her family donated that
econ building and that they never lost her money. Or else

why did she never have to work, was able to spend so freely, etc.? Can't wait to discuss this with Annemarie, but she took an extra week of break to check out LA club scene. She picked a good week to be gone. My classes are impossible all of a sudden. Professors just realized that semester ends in 3 weeks and have shifted into some higher gear without warning. Papers due left and right, must read an entire book tonight.

Should have worked ahead like Mary Jo on Thanksgiving break. But was too busy watching TV with Ed, Eric, Dan, Peter, Jim . . . crap, still can't remember 6th name. Man Who Does Not Speak. Either Karsten or Horst or Soren or . . . Kierkegaard.

Saw Wittenauer tonight for the first time since bowling trip. Very awkward at first. He pulled me aside and said he couldn't stop thinking about one thing during break, it almost ruined his entire vacation back home in Iowa. I thought from the way he was looking at me, and the way he'd asked me out and I'd turned him down, he meant *me*. That he couldn't stop thinking about *me*. Got very uncomfortable and pretended that an alum was calling me back, grabbed the phone, etc.

But then he said, "I couldn't stop thinking about how I need to tell Dean Sobransky the truth. About how I need to out myself."

Nearly dropped my stack of index cards. Wittenauer is gay? I was thinking. I rejected him and now he is rejecting the female species? Or maybe he was *never* asking me out, and stupid me assumed, which was a very dumb assumption. "Well, yeah, there comes a time in a person's life, you know. Like my sister, Alison, she didn't come out of the closet until last year—"

Wittenauer rolled his eyes. "I was talking about coming out of the *costume*. I feel really guilty for hiding behind Corny. I feel like I'm being dishonest to Dean Sobransky, who deep down is a pretty good guy, by not telling him I'm behind the whole school change concept, plus I'm letting you take the flak, which isn't fair to *you*—"

Was trying to talk him down from the ledge, tell him not to stress so much, when Dean S. came into the offices. First he invited us all to an end-of-semester party at his house next Sunday night, the 10th, to thank us for all our hard work. Then he encouraged us all to make an extra push because people get more generous during the holiday season.

"Why don't you have us stand downtown in Santa suits, accepting quarters in a can?" I asked.

"Courtney, please," Dean S. said. "Do try to take this a little more seriously. Our future is at stake here. Alumni giving is down thirty-nine percent from last year." He pointed to the giant ear of corn on the wall that measures our fund drive. "The kernels should go up to here," he said, illustrating by pointing with a pool cue he was mysteriously carrying around. "They're way down here. What we have here is an undergrown ear of corn."

"Maybe it was genetically engineered," I suggested.

Everyone laughed—except Dean S. "This is a very serious matter. We need to up our endowment. Tell the alumni you reach that our endowment is slipping," Dean S. said.

"You want me to say that we're not well endowed?" Rachel asked. "You're kidding, right?" He wasn't.

Then he cornered me and said he hoped I had a nice Thanksgiving. And wasn't it nice that the seasons had changed, and football was over, and so that meant of course that my little protest group had ended for the season as well?

"But there's basketball teams, right? And hockey is really big here," I said. "Isn't it? Men's and women's teams? And then there's swimming—"

"Courtney! We're not changing the name of the college!" Dean S. cried, banging the pool cue against a file cabinet.

The whole time, Wittenauer staring at us, biting his nails, racked by guilt, not helping.

"We don't want you to change the name of the college," I said.

Dean S. looked at me as if I had just kissed him and offered to bear his children. Ugh. "You don't? Oh, well, then what do you want?" Smiled at me and looked very greedy all of a sudden, sort of like the Grinch.

Suddenly I realized I had no idea. Have not been spending any time on this lately, and lost my train of thought. "We, uh, want, um, our voices to be heard," I said.

"That can be arranged. I suppose," Dean S. said.

"When?" I asked.

"Let me get back to you on that." Sounded very much like he did not mean that at all.

Later on, Wittenauer made me promise I will go to the Badicals meeting this Sunday and asked me to bring anyone I can round up—Annemarie of course, and even Thyme. Told him that Thyme had been transformed/morphed into Morgan, that she is wearing makeup over neck tattoo and getting French manicures and enrolling in business classes for next semester. I told him that when I asked her what's going on with her, how she can just turn her back on her entire personality, she said, "I

241

realized I needed to be *in* the system to *fight* the system."

"How establishment is that? What *happened* to her?" I asked Wittenauer.

Thought he would laugh, but he didn't. "She's just like everyone else," he said bitterly. "You're really naïve if you think anyone actually cares about changing this place, or the world, or anything."

Whoa. Might go slip my Mental Health Resources brochure under Wittenauer's door. Only I can't remember where he lives exactly.

Told him not to stress out so much, that obviously there are people who care. So we're a little aimless right now, but we'll pull it together.

Feel like everyone around me is cracking under the pressure of coming exams and massive amounts of work. Mary Jo and Joe are not speaking due to some notes-borrowing misunderstanding. Tricia snapping at a customer for taking too many pennies from the "Take a Penny!" cup. Marcus showing up at work in ratty T-shirt; Ben studying at every spare moment and getting all the orders wrong.

Good thing I cracked 2 weeks before now and am able to be there for people. Mostly this means they yell at me.

I have not seen the sun for days. Keep expecting to see polar bears on my way to class. Instead, layers and layers of fleece pass by. Largest coats I have ever seen. Boots also.

I don't understand how people ended up settling here, how they survived, unless this is warmer than Scandinavia? Or do they have different skin from me, like animals who have evolved, adapted? I have definitely not adapted.

> Dear Mom,
> In case you are wondering what I might like
> for Christmas and if you can take a break from
> chat room and have time to shop on line, I
> could really use a new winter coat. Something
> large and thick and preferably not bright
> yellow or orange.
> In all seriousness, I hope things are going
> well, and I can't wait to see you in a couple of
> weeks.
> Love,
> Courtney
>
> Hi Courtney!
> I was on line when you wrote—not in a chat
> room, don't worry. It's so good to hear from
> you! I can't wait to see you at Christmastime.

I hope we can spend *lots* of time together. How
are things with Grant? Did you settle things?

Mom,
Everything with Grant is okay. I'm really too
busy here right now to even worry about that.

Yeah. Right.
Grant e-mailed me from computer lab tonight, where
he and Melinda are working on writing some big report.
Tried to tell myself this was no big deal, Mary Jo has a lab
partner, too. Joe. And they sleep together, so, you know,
what am I worried about???

Got Christmas card from Mary Jo's family today. Reminds me I still haven't sent thank-you note, and am in possession of world's worst manners.

December 1st. Christmas is coming up way too fast, like some high-speed bullet train. Usually it's the fallen-behind-on-shopping that gets to me. This year it's the . . . what is going to happen when I get home? Things with Grant seem okay, but we are not talking as often and I have flashes of jealousy when we do. Like for instance why does he *need* a lab partner? Melinda should partner up with someone else. Grant can do the work on his own, he's smart enough.

Perhaps Johannsens wouldn't mind 1 more mouth to feed at Christmas dinner, either. If they won't take me in, maybe Mary Jo's biological mother will. She might need help delivering all those Christmas cards and packages.

Spent the morning selling BF gift certificates and filling a display case with "Knockwurst Stockings" full of knockwurst treats for DOGS.

Need I say more?

Not now, because I already did at work. Tried to point out the contradiction this creates.

"You're saying that we're selling this prepackaged dog biscuit that is essentially made of the same things as our Knockwurst Knots, and this is supposed to send what kind of message to our customers?"

Strike 843 against me, but Courtney still not out.

Jennifer actually said, "Yeah. It's kind of gross when you stop and think about it."

Finally vindicated.

Not that it matters—we still sell the stuff.

Which is okay because I've got Oscar's Christmas present wrapped up now, for a discount.

Annemarie is back, and we went to the Badicals meeting today. It is our last one of the semester, because next Sunday is so-called Crunch Day, last day before finals begin. (Same day as Dean S.'s party. Why is he giving a party on a Sunday night before finals? Probably doesn't want a high turnout.)

At the meeting we talked about how we want to settle this whole CFC thing, and I said that Dean S. had promised to let our voice be heard. We made this list of our demands, and then decided to protest outside the bookstore on Saturday. They always give a lot of campus tours on Saturdays, for one thing. For another, everyone is jamming the bookstore now for study supplies, paper, highlighters, textbooks they never bought at the beginning of semester.

I think this is Crunch Month. I am going to spend the entire day studying. Annemarie, Mary Jo, Peña, and I are all sitting in the lounge, armed with pretzels and rice cakes, the low-fat study group.

Thyme just came by and asked what we talked about at our meeting. Annemarie said she should have come if she wanted to know. Didn't understand her hostility until she pointed out that we can't trust Thyme now. Morgan. Whoever. Because she's working against us now, and is only asking in order to infiltrate the group for her own good. That seems sort of unlikely. I bet she just misses hanging out with us.

Funny day at work. We put up more holiday decora-
tions—garlands of lacquered bagels—and then discussed
possible holiday specials. I said I wanted to do a Ginger-
spread Gingerbread bagel. (This job is either growing on
me—or growing in me, like a disease.) Marcus wanted to
have something called New Year's Cheese. Ben wanted to
have a Kwazy Kwanzaa Pizzaa, just for the visual of z's
and a's. I don't think he was being serious, I think he was
making fun of me and Marcus.

Anyway, Jennifer listened and seemed really interested and impressed. Then she announced that she had
just received her shipment of the company's holiday
menu items—on ice. She let out this sad sigh and brought
out the tray with the things on it. First the Merry Carver:
turkey rolled into a bagel. Then Rudolph's Roast Beef—
meat, bagel, the usual, only more bloody. "What next—
actual reindeer meat?" I asked. Then there were Sugar
Cookie bagels, which tasted very rude. And the Kris
Kringle Single, a nasty-looking green and white candy
thing that was supposed to be a dollar bill.

"This stuff makes even the Bacle look good," I said,
"which is saying a lot. I *really* don't think we can sell this
stuff. I don't think *I* can, anyway."

I waited for the inevitable strike 3. Maybe I wanted it
to come. Go ahead. Throw me out. I'll have more time to
study for finals.

But Jennifer said, "I agree, these things look terrible.

I bet we can come up with better ideas on our own."

"What? But we can't," Ben said. "We're not allowed."

"Wait—wait. Before we decide *anything*, are there holiday aprons?" Marcus asked.

Jennifer then announced a very amazing thing. Once every year, the managers are allowed to run their own specials. Jennifer said, "The time is now." She confessed that she's totally sick of answering to corporate headquarters, tired of all the unreasonable sales goals, tired of getting slammed with new products, etc., and was probably going to leave soon, but maybe this would revitalize her.

Then she insisted we work through the day, into the night, developing our ideas. Does she not understand the concept of burnout? But it was actually fun. When the store closed, we blasted music, made signs, experimented with recipes, etc.

Courtney's Gingerbread Spread. Coming soon to a non-chain near you.

Have been studying constantly, so I haven't been able to write in here much. However, 2 things are notable. The 1st one extremely notable.

1st Thing: Mary Jo broke up with Joe yesterday. For good this time, she promises. He kept showing up late or not showing up and then she saw him at the library with another girl and then he said he had to look at other options because she didn't care enough about him to bring him home for Thanksgiving, and she said if he couldn't understand why she did that then he'd never understand her, so what was the point? That I needed her more at the time. Whoa. As noted earlier: surprising amount of backbone.

2nd Thing: I got a Christmas card from Ed today. It was signed: "Love, Ed." "You didn't tell Ed any weird stories, did you?" I asked Mary Jo. "Like, that I broke up with Grant and I was interested in him?"

"No way," Mary Jo said. "But don't worry. He'll be totally infatuated with you for a few months, and then *poof*! He'll drop you and find someone else. He does this constantly."

Hope the infatuation ends soon. He's a very sweet person and all, but I don't really see myself ever liking him that way. Would have to get over my fear of flannel, for one thing.

Annemarie got me a spot on the radio today to discuss our CFC-logo cause. *Talking with Wauzataukie* is the show. Usually they pull some random person off the street and interview them. The DJ, named Paul, asked me to describe my pet issue.

"I don't have a pet *issue*," I said. "I do have a dog named Oscar, though, and I love him very much." Was supposed to just be a little joke, but we got into this lengthy discussion of our dogs and how weird Oscar is and how funny his Chihuahua is. Suddenly I realized my time was almost up and I hadn't done anything to promote our cause.

Might be fired as organizer of this thing. Managed at the last second to get in our plug for the protest tomorrow at the bookstore, but might have been cut off mid-sentence.

Oh well. Nobody listens to the campus station anyway. Right?

Attacked! I've been attacked!

Went to the CFC bookstore. There's this lobby area with lockers to stash backpacks—a couple of tables that are usually filled with people selling Guatemalan sweaters and credit cards.

Erik and I and a few other Badicals set up a table with signs, banners, posters, etc. We were sitting there greeting people and handing out a flyer about how we want new sweatshirts, new notebooks, new bumper stickers, etc. We had brought all these cans with symbols that said "no CFCs" to remind everyone of what a *negative image* we're promoting here.

We kept trying to grab people as they went in and out of the bookstore. This big group of students came toward us, and I got hopeful because there were a lot of Phish T-shirts and reggae colors and green army pants in the crowd. So I stepped toward them to make my pitch.

All of a sudden, out of nowhere, someone jumped right in front of me and sprayed something all over me. I was seeing red. I thought I was bleeding. "What are you doing?" I demanded, reaching for the sleeve of his jacket. "Stop it!"

"This is really lame and useless!" the sprayer yelled. "Why don't you work on something meaningful for a change? Fight for change that matters! Do something important!"

"I am!" I yelled, pawing at the wool ski mask the man

was wearing—like half the people around here do just to walk to class. Not good evidence.

I wiped off my face and saw this stuff on my hand that looked like blood. It turned out to be watered-down ketchup.

"People are dying every day, and you're arguing over *sweatshirts?*" he yelled. "Forget bumper stickers. Save someone's life!" He ran off, leaving us to get into a fight with bookstore staff over who should clean up the mess.

Protest over. Game over. We collected all our stuff and went home and everyone stared at me as I walked across campus as if I had been shot. Mary Jo clung to me when I walked in the door, ready to call 911, screaming, "Who did this? Who did this?" over and over.

Took a very long shower and thought things through. First I was very irate and mad. Sort of freaked out, also. Hate being criticized. Then I realized masked man is right.

It's not exactly a serious cause, but we had good environmental intentions at the beginning. We need to wrap this up and move on to another, more serious issue.

I wonder what group he was from. Or was he sent by Dean S. to break up our protest? I've got to ask Wittenauer about it tomorrow at the party at Dean S.'s house. If he goes. If I go.

Okay, so how many parties have I gone to that I shouldn't have?

Well, 1 good outcome. 1 very unsettling outcome.

First: Wittenauer and I tracked down Dean S. by the "nacho hot dish." Looked like nachos to me. He had lots of food and a giant bowl of cider on a table by the fireplace. Roaring fire, very cozy, festive, if you could ignore Wisconsin sports memorabilia clogging the living room.

Dean S. said he heard about the bookstore melee yesterday and that he wants to resolve this peacefully. "So do I!" I said. "So could we please set a date for us to talk to the administration?"

"You can bring all your concerns to the trustee meeting on January fifth," Dean S. offered.

"But classes don't start until the eighth. You're only scheduling it then because most people don't get back until the seventh!" I said.

"You can come back early," Dean S. said. "Of course, if you're not really committed to this . . . " He looked very hopeful.

I picked up another nacho, scraped some beef off of it, and ate it. "Oh, I'm committed," I said. Or I should be.

Dean S. turned to serve another guest some punch, and Wittenauer started to get this really antsy look. "I have to tell him. I'm going to tell him," Wittenauer said.

"Don't!" I whispered. "It's better if you work behind the scenes. Behind the helmet, I mean."

254

"Why is that better?" he asked.

"Because you can, um, get closer to people," I said. That came out entirely wrong.

"I can?" Wittenauer asked.

"You could like, infiltrate conversations," I said. "Stay friends with Dean S. and figure out what the administration is planning."

"But that would make me a spy," he said.

"I know. Isn't it cool?" I said.

Just then Dean S. turned around. "Well, Walter? What are you planning for your vacation?"

"Not much. But there's something I want to tell you before we all leave for break," Wittenauer said.

"Don't!" I said as I grabbed his arm.

Wittenauer smiled. "I was only going to tell him what an excellent fund-raiser you are. She's made a real contribution to the group, you know, Dean Sobransky?"

"Er . . . yes." Dean Sobransky obsessively filling cups with the exact same amount of cider. 30 cups teetering on the table. He did not realize the cider was sort of beyond its date and had morphed into an alcoholic beverage. Within the hour carols were being sung and Dean S. was nervously and discreetly arranging rides home for all of us.

Wittenauer walked me back to Rankin. We were standing outside and laughing about the stuff in Dean S.'s house and about exams starting tomorrow and how we were sort of tipsy.

Mary Jo walked by on her way home from the science

library and glared at us as she went by. Apparently didn't approve of partying on nights before exams. Probably right.

"So Courtney? Have a really good vacation," Wittenauer said. "Don't forget to work on our arguments for the trustee meeting, and call me if you need any help. It was great hanging out with you tonight. And thanks for keeping me from confessing to being Corny."

"Well. You're kind of blowing your cover right now. You're being *very* corny," I said.

Wittenauer rolled his eyes. "Ha ha. Good night." Then he kissed me on the cheek. Felt very sophisticated. And I thought, Cool! That's what friends do in college.

But then he kissed me again—on the lips. For real. And the kiss just, like, blew me away, because I haven't kissed anyone that intensely since Grant. And it seemed very romantic because it was sort of snowing, little ice crystals were falling on our cheeks, and we were leaving for vacation, and we were standing there smushed up against each other and it felt warm—

Then I realized I was doing *exactly* what Grant did to me. Getting totally carried away by the proximity of a good-looking, opposite-sex friend and a couple of cups of turned cider!

"So, okay, good night," I said, bolting for the safety of the dorm.

"Courtney, would you *please* stop that?" Mary Jo just asked, interrupting flow of thought here. She is still studying. "You're humming. Or glowing. Or *something*."

"Sorry," I said. "I was just thinking about something."

"Like how you and Walter were making out? And how you're going to tell Grant about it when you get home on Friday? Or maybe you should call him now, and get it over with—"

Whoa! "We weren't making out," I said. "It was a friendly kiss. A kiss between friends. And his name isn't Walter."

"Please. I could see you guys from up here," she said. "And if you're trying to get revenge on Grant or something by using Walter—"

"His name is Wittenauer!" I interrupted. "Only teachers are allowed to call him Walter."

"—then in a way you don't deserve Grant, who drove all the way out here to beg your forgiveness, and who's going to fail out of college if you don't totally forgive him soon—"

"So he fails?" I said. "So what?"

But the thought of Grant never becoming a D.V.M., never opening Superior Animal Hospital, is very upsetting. I don't want that. Don't want to make out with WW III again. I kissed a school mascot. *Voluntarily.* I really need to get out of here. Christmas can't come soon enough.

Exams start today.
      I go home on Friday.
      Wish me luck.
      See you then.
      Yes, I should tell Grant what happened.
      But am too busy worrying. I mean studying.

On the plane right now. Direct from Milwaukee to Denver. Feeling very jittery. Spent last 3 nights awake due to 1) cramming for exams, 2) anxiety attacks, 3) camping out at library overnight last night so I wouldn't see Ed when he came to pick up Mary Jo for Christmas. Man does not take "no" for an answer, kept insisting I spend Christmas on the farm, Christmas riding horse and sleigh, Christmas as Mrs. Ed.

I'm writing to look busy because the 2 people next to me keep talking, trading "Best Christmas Ever" and "Worst Christmas Ever" stories. Since I'm thinking this year will be one or the other, I don't want to get involved.

Oh no. We're beginning our descent.

Funny, I thought I began my descent about a month ago. Ha ha ha.

I am so nervous. I can't even think about the fact I just took 4 finals and don't know how I did. I can't finish my soda and the flight attendant is getting really annoyed because he keeps coming by to get everyone's cups and I'm sorry but it's like *too much pressure* right now for me to finish my diet 7-Up.

All I can think about is that Grant is picking me up at the airport and I'm going to die when I see him.

LATER...

Home. In bed. Exhausted. Oscar's furry chin is resting on my shin.

Grant wasn't at the airport.

NOT AN OMEN NOT AN OMEN NOT AN OMEN

Bryan was.

He said that Grant called in a panic because he couldn't get out of work due to the holiday crush/rush and could Bryan please pick me up, he was really sorry blah blah blah.

I was starting to get furious by the baggage carousel when Bryan handed me a present Grant had dropped by the house already as a "Welcome Home" gift (a/k/a Forgive Me). I opened this little box and inside was a pair of silver earrings with little amber stones that match my hair. Beautiful. But does he think earrings will fix everything? I wondered as I lugged my giant Army duffel of Christmas presents off the conveyor belt. If I'd never bought all this stuff for Grant when I was still in love with him, I wouldn't have bounced checks and maxed out new credit card.

Am I still in love with him? You can't have these thoughts at airports under fluorescent lights while avoiding Smarte Cartes and listening to overhead pages.

Anyway, Bryan asked if I was hungry, which I was, now that I wasn't worried about seeing Grant tonight, so we went to Perkins on the way home. An amazing thing happened there. Over a pitcher of coffee and way too many pancakes, we had our first real, actual conversation ever. Mind blowing. He told me about Mom and his theory of why she won't date the guy in the book club or the guy from the awards banquet and will only write flirty e-mails to men in cyberspace. If they are actually men, and not a) 15-year-old boys or b) women.

He told me about this girl he's seeing now, Samantha, and his theory of why they're good together. Turns out he has many theories, even about me, Grant, and especially Beth. He isn't bitter at all. Not sure where he got that from.

But here is the mind-blowing fact of the evening: *he* broke up with Beth. Not the other way around. He said he was pretty sure she didn't see it coming, thought she could just treat him like he was always going to be there for her, no matter what. She was totally shocked and upset. So maybe that's why she made such a huge mistake with Grant.

I felt myself starting to forgive Beth, right then and there, in the middle of Perkins at 11 P.M. Or was it just the maple syrup going to my head?

"Are you guys ever going to get back together?" I asked. Because that would make everything a whole lot easier for me.

"We might," Bryan said. "But I doubt it. Not right now, anyway. I could see maybe in another year, you know . . . "

Danger. Little brother starting to sound like ex Dave, with time theories. Next thing you know he will want to be "free and clear."

Got home and really really wanted to call Grant. Everything here is about him, about us. Except Mom knocking on my door, constantly asking if I need anything else. Driving me crazy.

Saw Grant for the first time this morning. Got so nervous, I tripped coming down the stairs. Not the impression I wanted to make. We hugged, then stood in the hallway for a minute or two. Very awkward. Still 100 percent attracted to Grant. Grant seems to think everything is A-okay between us, like isn't it great I'm home and now we can spend the next 2–3 weeks together? I'm just confused.

We went out to lunch and talked nonstop about school, classes, exams, papers, anything but about us. Then out of the blue he said, "What do you want to do for our anniversary?"

Anniversary?

"Well, that won't be until, um . . . " Until I figure out whether you can count the last month or not, since weren't we technically not together???

"New Year's," Grant said. "Right? So do you want to go skiing at Breckenridge like last year, or . . . "

"Sure," I said quickly. "Sure. Breckenridge. Sounds great."

He gave me a funny look and then went ahead and ordered dessert. It was so good to be with him again, but I didn't know if I could sit through an apple cobbler without crying. Also, I kept thinking that I had to tell him that I fell off the wagon, too, kissing WW III.

Kissing WW III. Yet *another* great name for a band.

Should probably give up pursuit of poli sci degree

and go into band management.

This working-things-out thing is so tedious. No wonder Dad just left, moved out of the house, started a new relationship without patching things up with Mom. Perhaps I don't give him enough credit for being smart.

Talked to Mom today about her perennial singleness. Kept tossing out names of potential suitors. "Whatever happened with that nice single guy you met at the awards ceremony? The father of that girl Bryan likes? You guys really hit it off. So why won't you go out with him?"

She beat around the bush for like 20 minutes talking about Christmas week/tree trimming/dinner plans. Then she finally said, "But he drives a Saturn. Two-door."

"*So?*" I asked.

"Well, I've never liked anyone who drove a coupe. Man or woman." She said this like it was logical.

Grrrr. She's going to spend the rest of her life all alone because she'd rather get involved with a sedan person? Or worse—another mini-van driver, to match her Caravan?

"So what *are* you looking for, Mom? An SUV?" I asked.

She wouldn't answer. She got all offended.

"Mom, come on, I'm worried about you," I said. "Alison and I are both in college, and Bryan's going to be soon—"

"So what are you saying? I'm old? Yes, I know I'm old, thanks for pointing that out."

"Mom, you're only . . . what? Forty-three?"

"Forty-seven."

"Oh." That seems old, but I didn't tell her that.

Totally embarrassing scene tonight.

Grant came over to get me so we could go Christmas shopping at the new giant mall in Broomfield. Went to our favorite stores but didn't buy anything. Felt really uncomfortable. Whenever he took my hand to hold it, I started thinking horrible things about how I kissed Wittenauer and hadn't 'fessed up yet. So there we were, strolling through the food court, when I heard someone yelling my name. Turned around and saw the Tom coming toward us. Agh! So humiliating. The last time I *saw* him was months ago, and the last time I talked to him, he was telling me how Grant and Beth hooked up. And like gloating about it.

The Tom came toward us doing his trademark saunter, like he didn't really *care* if we were there or not, even though he was shouting my name sort of desperately a couple of seconds ago. He had 2 girls with him, of course—never travels without at least 2. They looked like they might be high-school sophomores. Maybe. So he gave me this hug that was verging on pornographic, the girls looked mad, Grant looked pissed, never mind there's never been *anything* between me and Tom and never will be. Then he stood back and said "Hey, Superior," and then he said, "So you *are* still together." Sounded very shocked. Not that it takes much to puzzle the Tom, but still. Had he heard otherwise?

Stopped by T or D today to visit Gerry and bring him a block of Wisconsin brick cheese. Drove up to buffalo overlook first to visit old friends and prepare myself, just in case. Then I drove to Canyon Blvd. and sat outside in the car trying to establish that Beth was definitely not inside T or D, not in the storeroom, not in the bathroom, not out back smoking. . . . I must have been there 20 minutes. People kept going in and coming out with their smoothies and sundaes. They'd come back to their cars and see me sitting there, and I knew it was only a matter of time before 1 of them reported me for being a stalker.

Also I started to feel like a freak, sitting there parked outside my old workplace. Like I couldn't move on or something. Hey, I have moved on. I don't even live here anymore.

Finally got out of the car and went into the store. On the way in, checked out strip-mall sign that Beth had supposedly damaged. Looked fine to me. Went inside. Gerry wasn't there. Place was very crowded. Out of control. Beth working. Very flustered. 1 woman was complaining about her sundae having the wrong syrup, a boy was demanding a cleaner spoon, etc. Meanwhile there were about 10 people waiting for smoothies and cones. Beth caught my eye and her face sort of brightened. Her hair was all askew and she had 10 different fruits splashed on her hemp apron. I just felt so *bad*. We'd been in this situation together so many times.

So the next thing I knew I was dashing behind the counter, grabbing the apron covered with the Holstein cow pattern. "Don't you hate these balmy December days where everyone feels they just *have* to get out and enjoy frozen food products?" I muttered to Beth as I quickly washed my hands.

We got to work really quickly and didn't speak much for the next half hour. When I looked up and there was no line, I knew we'd have to talk. Busied myself making my own smoothie while I stalled. My old favorite, a CFS. That's CF for Coconut Fantasy, not Cornwall Falls. Not to be confused. Ever.

Beth came over to stand beside me. "Thanks for coming to my rescue. How did you know Gerry ran out for supplies right *before* the after-lunch rush?"

"I didn't." Because if I had, I wouldn't have come in here, I thought. But I had to be more "mat-oor" about all this. "Um, I just thought we should talk," I said.

"So, when did you get home?" she asked.

"Saturday," I said. "Well, Friday, but late." We made small talk for a while, about Jane, about Christmas plans, about exams. Then there was this gulf that opened up. I wanted her to bring up the Grant thing. I wanted a customer to come in and order 10,000 smoothies, so neither one of us would have to bring it up. But it was good to see her, even if my stomach was bubbling like overcooked hot fudge. You know when you take it off the burner but it keeps cooking. Like that.

"You never answered any of my e-mails," she finally

said. "And that's okay. But I just—well, it's been kill-ing me."

"Me, too," I said.

"I don't know, Court," she said. "I don't think you should forgive me. But if you could . . . that would be so great."

Just then Gerry barreled through the door carrying packages of napkins and a tower of boxes of plastic sil-verware. He was panting and out of breath. He stared at me, did a double take, and then dropped one of the boxes. It opened as it fell, and 100 plastic forks spilled onto the tile floor.

"Now, what am I going to do with a hundred forks?" he muttered. "I can't believe I grabbed forks by mistake. Courtney? I don't know why you have an apron on, but a little help? Please?"

I went over and started collecting them into a heap. "You're going to have to wash these now, you realize."

"Not to mention come up with menu items requiring forks." He laughed. "How are you? When did you get into town?"

"A few days ago," I said. "I came by to bring you something, and, well. You know. The after-lunch rush was happening."

He stood up and brushed some chocolate sprinkles off his knees. "Well, I guess I didn't need to rush back. You guys have everything covered, as usual."

I helped him carry the stuff into the storeroom while

Beth waited on customers. After we put the spoons and napkins on shelves, he stood there and stared at me for a few seconds, doing his typical Gerry "let me analyze you because I used to do this for a living" gaze.

"Your hair . . . you're different," he said. I had sort of forgotten about my haircut. Least of my problems lately. Also, I keep forgetting that I have these 2 separate lives now—home and school.

"Everything's going all right at school?" he asked.

"Um, sure," I said. "I mean, as well as can be expected."

That scared him. "You're not flunking out, are you?"

"No, of course not," I said.

"And you and Grant, you're doing well?" he asked.

"As well as can be expected," I said again. Trying to give him an answer without really answering. Only way to deal with prying questions.

"So. Everything going all right with, you know?" He tried to make a sly little head gesture toward Beth, who was still up front.

"Sure," I said. "I mean . . . as well as can be expected."

"Is that what you're going to say to all my questions from now on?" he asked, giving me the old G.C. look.

"Pretty much," I said.

Left with the promise to call Beth tomorrow and possibly meet her and Jane, who gets in tonight after trip to see new bf's band perform in Chicago.

I hope Beth and I can put this behind us and move on and be friends again. I have really missed her. Am crossing my fingers as I write this. With my other hand, dummy.

Spent a hilarious afternoon at Jane's house. Jane and I were telling Wisconsin stories to Beth, exaggerating maybe a little, but mostly true. Talked about stupid things we'd done at parties and said in class. Reminisced about senior year. I described seeing the Tom at the mall. Started telling Tom stories. We started giggling and couldn't stop. Perhaps it was because we were splitting beers stolen from the giant Nakamura beer fridge in the basement, while Jane played a tape of her new bf's music. I kept suggesting new names for his band but she wasn't impressed. I think maybe Brat Virgin stands a chance, though.

At one point I looked at Beth and realized I have to forgive her. Or I have already forgiven her. Like today. We have this connection. We have a history. It has nothing to do with Grant. Started thinking of how Mary Jo chose me over Joe, and how that talk show guest chose ho's over bro's.

And anyway, Beth spent like half an hour describing new guy she's seeing. So that helped.

I got home really late and Bryan said Grant had stopped by and called a couple of times and was looking kind of worried. We were supposed to go to dinner tonight. We were?

Alison got home yesterday. Very excited to see her. Spent all day and night talking. She has many valuable insights into . . . everything.

Why am I the only child in the family without insights? Is it because I'm the middle child? I'm too busy trying to convince everyone to get along to have insights. Despite insightful natures, however, Alison has only been home 24 hours and she and Bryan have already had 3 fights re: fabric softener sheets, folding stuff left in the dryer, and the lint screen.

Got a big package in the mail this afternoon. I thought it was from Mary Jo because of the return address, and I was completely shocked because we sort of exchanged little gifts before we left. But it wasn't from her. It was from Ed.

Grant happened to come over to get me just as I was opening the box and pulling out little red and green boxes with gold ribbons. (Really need to send those gifts back without opening them, but I wonder what they are.)

Grant looked very shocked. Stunned, actually.

"Who's *Ed*?" he asked in this really unhappy voice.

"Oh, just this guy," I said. "Mary Jo's brother."

"What? I don't believe you," Grant said.

"Look." I showed him the postmark and for a split second thought fondly of Mary Jo's bio mother, stamping the package. Pictured all the Johannsens, pictured the house, remembered the cows.

Grant misinterpreted my thoughtful moment as wistful pining. "Is that why you went to her house for Thanksgiving?" he asked. "So you could spend time with her brother Ed?"

"What?" I laughed. "No!" I started to describe how Ed and I got to know each other during Parents Weekend—

"You never mentioned that," Grant said. "You never said anything about Ed."

Then I realized how dangerously close we were getting to the WW III discussion, so I told him Ed was not important to me, it was a harmless crush, and that we'd better get going if we wanted to see the Wildlights at the Zoo.

Last year we kissed for the first time, okay actually sort of made out, at Wildlights. This year we stomped around in the cold with Grant not in a good mood, and I finally dragged it out of him that he found out he did not get all A's and actually got one B. Not even in his major, so who cares? But Grant cares. Obsessing about it. Tried to distract him with kisses. Was like kissing one of the metal giraffe statues.

'Twas the night before Christmas
And all through the house
Courtney was in big trouble

No more parties. *Really*. I mean it this time.

The big party was tonight. The Lebeau Mansion.

Last year I panicked and kissed the Tom. This year was even worse. Started out sort of fun, and also funny, because ex Dave showed up, home for Christmas. Gave him a huge hug and he looked confused. Didn't want to tell him he was right about LDRs being impossible, but he was. Not going to tell him that due to the rude way he dropped the bomb on me seconds before leaving town last year, that it was all over between us. Would never do that to anyone.

Anyway, here's what happened after that. Had some punch with Jane and Beth. Bryan and Alison were mingling. Grant and I then sat by the fire on this giant velvet sofa. Should have been very romantic but my mind kept wandering. I kept thinking about the fireplace at Dean S.'s house, our Fun-Times Funders party, and then I started thinking about Wittenauer, and my guilt about kissing him, and our trustee meeting coming up. Kept slugging punch. Grant and I went to refill our cups, and there was the Tom, hanging out with Beth. The Tom said something like, "Here comes the happy couple, back together again!" Beth looked like she wanted to die, and bolted for the front door. Didn't faze the Tom. He started teasing me all about how I was the forgiving type, and just his luck, he never got to go out with *those* kinds of girls. Then I told him that was because he only went out with idiot skanks.

Ran outside onto the terrace. Grant came outside after me. I threw my cup of punch over the cute brick wall and told him that I wasn't over what happened, was never going to get over it, couldn't stand that he kissed Beth and that I kissed Wittenauer and—

"What?" Grant said. "Who's Wittenauer?"

"His name's Walter, okay? And he's also Corny. And he's also a three," I said. "And let's face it. He just doesn't sound as good as he is in person."

"What?" Grant cried again. "Courtney, who is this guy? Are you serious about him?"

"No! We're friends, that's all," I said. "And it didn't mean anything, we just got carried away by a Badicals project and we were at this party and he walked me home and it just *happened*."

"You've been home for a week, and you're just telling me now?" Grant went into furious mode. "Court, I called you the next day after Beth and I . . . you know. And that's only because I was waiting until it was a decent hour—"

"Like there's a decent hour to tell me that you and my best friend—"

"It was nothing! Nothing nothing nothing!" Grant insisted.

We got into this competition of whose slip-up/kiss error was worse, mine or his. Practically screaming. Completely ridiculous.

Went inside and got Bryan and insisted he take me home right away. The Tom overheard and volunteered to drive me.

"I have enough problems, okay? I don't need you mauling me in the car," I said.

"Like I would," the Tom said.

Not *this* again.

Still haven't heard from Grant since last night. I haven't called him, either. Christmas Stalemate.

Mom is losing her mind. Wonder if she has that seasonal disorder, because it seems like every winter she goes a bit berserk. Spending way too much money on Christmas. Last year she got us all cell phones, but then decided they were no better than traditional phones and returned them. This year she got us all new iBooks because the Internet is her life and thinks it should be ours, too.

"Hey, no complaints, I'll give my other computer to Mary Jo. But Mom. I'm sort of worried," I said. It's like she thinks this is her revenge against the phone company, to live through DSL. Not a life, I pointed out. Alison and I gave long lecture about perils of Instant Messaging with pedophiles. Or in her case, middle-age-o-philes.

There are always people on talk shows, where it's a 25-year-old dude dating a 50-year-old mom he met through Internet. Lives rent-free, giant scam. Sorry Mom, but we're the only ones allowed to live rent-free here.

We gave her a really hard time. We went on and on with endless examples of how she shouldn't trust anybody. Ever. Needless to say, I led the crusade.

Then she told us the guy she's going out with on New Year's is the guy in town, from the awards ceremony. And could we please just shut up? She learned her lesson already about chat rooms, and was only trying to give us these computers so we'd have the best advantage in school, in the world . . . Oops.

Alison gave me a cool sweater, Bryan gave me CDs, Dad sent cash. Typical Christmas, really. I'm sort of glad Dad & Sophia & Angelina & Bellarina didn't come, because last year it was so crowded. Grandma and Grandpa should get here tonight. I'm sure Grandpa will have a million questions about Cornball and I'll have to put my game face on, tell him I love it.

Well, at least I don't *hate* it anymore. There is that.

LATER . . .

Grant is back to being Superior.

I was sitting by the window, watching for Grandma and Grandpa, when I saw his car pull up. Nearly had a heart attack. Resisted urge to run upstairs and hide under comforter. Tried to be an adult and went to open the door. Grant came in. He started babbling apologies, and I started trying to counter each apology with one of my own. Then we just looked at each other and I started crying and we started hugging. Grant put his arms around my waist and started kissing my neck. And somehow everything was okay again. Like we're even now or something.

Ditched waiting for my grandparents to show up and went over to Grant's house. Very warm reception, parents and Grandmother Superior thrilled to see me. Then they disappeared upstairs so Grant and I could be alone.

Christmas carols were playing softly on the stereo. We were holding hands, leaning against each other on sofa. Then suddenly Grant got up and kneeled down, on bended knee or however you say that.

I started panicking. He was going to propose! Mary Jo said we should get engaged if we were serious. But we'd only truly made up a couple of hours ago. What was I going to do, say, how should I react?

Then he scooted across the carpet. Turned out he was just getting down on the floor to pull my presents out from under the tree.

Gave me a new watch, very cool, with a note about counting minutes until we're together this summer. Gave me a coupon book with all these coupons he'd designed for my favorite things, like: One Chauffeured Drive to Buffalo Overlook, One Hot Dog with the Works at Mustard's Last Stand, etc.

Love Grant. Love love love him.

Am not going back to CFC for spring semester. Staying here, transferring to CU. Must stay with Grant. I could work full time. Make tons of money; ski every weekend; see Grant all the time. Beautiful plan.

"So you didn't make the Dean's List," Grandpa said when I got up this morning and stumbled downstairs for coffee. "Is that what you're telling me?"

"Um, well, I'm not sure yet, because I haven't gotten my grades." I did make Dean S.'s list of "People He'd Like to See Transfer from CFC." Did that count?

Then he cleared his throat and said he heard about my little protest idea to change the CFC "image." We got into a big debate, discussion, whatever. He said our idea was "needless nitpicking."

"But it's so simple," I said. "They could add graduate programs and become Cornwall Falls University. CFU. That would work," I said.

"Don't you get it?" Grandma said. "Initials aren't everything in this world, Courtney!"

This from the woman whose family gave me the middle initials V.D.!!!

Total cold war inside house now. He and Grandma are furious with me. Mom, however, is proud of me for being so involved. I guess she didn't know that I was actually having an impact. Never gives me credit for having an impact on anything.

Told Alison and Bryan I am thinking about not going back to Wisconsin next week. They told me I'm crazy. Alison said that would be like taking a giant step backward, because my credits might not transfer and I'd be a freshman next fall, and wasn't once enough? She had a billion arguments about how this would ruin my future academic life, my career, the possibility of me ever becoming Anybody.

Bryan took different tack. He said not to make any decisions based on love. (Has obviously been watching too many relationship experts on *Oprah*, which Mom *tapes* and watches during dinner, exposing her only son to dangerous airborne chemical: talk shows.) (I watch enough to know how they suck you in and ruin your own personal ozone layer.) He said I'd always feel I made a big sacrifice for Grant, and how I'd never be happy.

Hey, I can *be* happy, with or without Grant.

Wait a second. What am I saying?

Was being stupid and paranoid today and called Grant to ask him if our anniversary ski date is still on. Of course it is, and then he got mad at me for doubting the date, doubting him, me, etc.

"Okay, so I was thinking about moving back here for you, and you're going to get mad at me now?" I asked.

"What?" he said. "You were going to . . . ?"

"Never mind," I said. "See you tomorrow, okay?"

"How can you move back *here* when I'm planning to drive you back *there*?" Grant asked.

"What? You are?" (Is he trying to get rid of me?)

We discussed the plan—to leave on Tuesday, get there early in the morning on Wednesday. He doesn't have to come back until Saturday, so that will give us 3 days together. Plus he can be there for the trustee meeting.

So sweet of him.

But the idea makes me very very nervous. Like TV movie of the week: *Grant in Wauzataukie: When 2 Worlds Collide!*

Spent the day trying to convince Jane to drive back with me and Grant instead of waiting for silly first-class flight in a week.

"No way, I'm not going back yet!" Jane said. "Are you crazy?"

"But you do love Madison," I reminded her. "And Charles is there, right?"

"No, he's home with his family, too," she said.

"Oh. Well, aren't you getting tired of living under your parents' roof? I mean, it's driving *me* crazy, because I'm not used to having my mom watch my every move, you know?"

"My parents are cool. They sort of let me live my own life," Jane said. She took off her little rectangular glasses to clean them. "What's really going on here, Courtney?" she asked.

I shrugged. "Nothing. I just thought it would be fun, that's all. Road trip. Loud music. Windows down."

"It's winter," she said. "And you're still not telling me what's at the root of your question."

Does she *have* to major in psych? "I don't know what you mean," I said. When in doubt, feign ignorance.

"Why do you want me there? Don't you want to be alone with Grant?" Jane asked.

Busted. I twirled around on the kitchen stool. "Well, actually, um, *no*."

"Courtney, you have to be alone with him sooner or

later," Jane said. "He's coming to college to stay with you for a few days. Do you really think you can delay it by having me in the backseat? And anyway, what's wrong? Why can't you face spending sixteen hours in a car with him? Is there something you haven't told me?"

So I told her about our big fight, and how I cheated with Wittenauer by kissing him. She was really excited about it, for some reason. "I don't understand. I thought you liked Grant," I said.

"I do!" she said. "But this means you've *individuated*. Which is what you have to do in order to move on and grow by yourself."

Don't know what she was talking about. I told her how we've worked through the problems and patched things up, but now I feel like one of those old roads with too many patched potholes. More patch than road.

She said I was being pessimistic, and that every relationship has problems, and the key is to get beyond the superficial problems (kissing others) to the root of the problem (mother issues). Well, sure. Anyone named Mrs. Superior is *going* to have issues. But does Grant have issues with that? Do I? Do I want to marry someone and be known to the world as Courtney Superior?

Wait a second. We are not discussing marriage, we are discussing a boring car trip on interstates. And anyway, Jane's had like 2 courses and thinks she can diagnose us?

"Okay," she said when I protested. "So what do you think? Is being exclusive going to work for you this semester any better than it did last semester?"

Did she have to ask that?

He's coming to pick me up soon to go out to dinner.
I should really think about getting dressed up.

Grant and I had a great day skiing. Last night we went out for an expensive dinner in LoDo with our Christmas money. Very nice, but that's not the big story. The big story is *Mom's first date in 5 years*!!!

This guy, Bryan's girlfriend's dad (easier to just say "Michael"), came to pick Mom up last night. In dreaded Saturn coupe. It was dark, so maybe Mom was more inclined to overlook his car choice. Mom was more dressed up than I've seen her since my high-school graduation. Looked beautiful. I took pictures like it was prom.

She got home *after* me, for once. (Grant and I came home pre-midnight and watched the ball drop on TV; he left as soon as she got home because it was 1 A.M.). Her face was shiny and happy. She started telling me about the place they went for dinner and how nice it was, and how Michael was really interesting, funny, devoted to his 2 daughters, etc. Then she burst out crying.

"Mom, what is it?" I asked. "What's wrong?"

"I can't explain," she said. "You wouldn't understand."

Just like Bryan! Assuming I won't get it, when truth is I get *everything*, and more.

"What happened?" I asked. "Did he say something? Was the coupe too small? Did he kiss wrong?"

She shook her head and ran for a Kleenex box. "It was all perfect. It was great. I had a really good time."

I just stood there next to her for a minute, waiting for

my brain to figure out what there was to cry about. Is Mom just sort of . . . unbalanced? Allergic to happiness?

"Tonight I realized what I've been missing," she finally said. "And it's wonderful. And it's horrible at the same time. You know?"

Agh! Why do relationships have to be so painful to everyone, like, all the time?

Why have one at all?

Tonight we are having a big family dinner: I leave tomorrow, Alison leaves Wednesday. Beth is coming over with Jane.

Sitting beside Grant in the car. Halfway back to WI. Landscape desolate and cold. We left at 6 A.M. so we can get there by midnight or so. Very hard saying good-bye to everyone last night. But not as hard as it was in August. It's better, I think, to know what you're about to get yourself back into than to get into it the first time. Like cold lake water.

Speaking of Lake Superior, I keep glancing over at Grant and smiling. I am so glad he's doing this with me? But in some ways, Mom was an easier traveling companion. Sad but true.

Agh! Disaster.

Grant and I slept late. We were finally heading out when suddenly Mary Jo arrived. She came back early to get a jump on her classes—of course. It was so nice to see her. We gave each other a big hug, and I was introducing her to Grant, and they were of course instantly hitting it off, laughing about his 2 trips out here, commiserating over each getting one B (tragedy).

So we were chatting outside our room as Mary Jo stood there with a suitcase in one hand and a new, horrid framed print in the other hand (a kitten and a puppy having tea) when Ed came down the hallway. At the moment, Grant was teasing me about something, like how I described this place as being *so* bad, but it was all I talked about while I was home, so he was sort of like pretending to give me a giant squeeze.

Before I knew what was happening, Ed ran up and punched Grant in the jaw! God. What a mess. Grant's already got one half-broken tooth. I could just picture another flying out of his mouth, and then I would be dating a hockey player.

Ed misunderstood the situation and told Grant to get his hands off of me. He told Grant he wasn't a real man because of what he did to me. (!) (Have never thought of Grant as "real man"—don't even know what that *means*.) Meanwhile Grant pushed him against the wall and was demanding to know why Ed was sending me gifts and what right he had to interfere, and Ed spat back that it was his right ever since I showed up at their house after Grant abandoned me.

The few girls on the floor who are already back came running out of their rooms to see what was going on. Mary Jo was shrieking at Ed to stop hurting Grant. I was yelling at both of them to just shut up, the whole time thinking: This *isn't* my life. Guys *don't* fight over me.

Some guys from downstairs, including R.A. Kevin, overheard, came running upstairs to break up the fight. Kevin made Ed and Grant shake hands and asked if they couldn't just talk it out, or maybe they should go back to their dorms or to a conflict resolution workshop at the housing office—

At which point Grant and Ed both said at the same time, "Hey, I don't even go here."

And that was sort of funny so it broke the ice. So we all went inside and sat in the room and made small talk. Still very awkward. Ed was sad because I tried to return his Christmas gifts; he wouldn't take them; said I should keep them and think of him from time to time. (Sounded like a country song.) Then he left to drive home.

Grant was upset that his jaw is bruised, and upset that Ed feels that possessive of me, and made me explain 10 times that Ed means nothing to me. Mary Jo helped by explaining this habit of crushes Ed has. Mary Jo, Grant, and I went to Brat W. for dinner. Someone working there actually *recognized* Grant. Mary Jo and Grant really did have a ton to talk about. And every once in a while I'd catch myself feeling jealous and suspicious, and then I'd just hate myself for it. But I couldn't stop.

Mary Jo is being sweet and spending the night down the hall in Tricia's room. Tricia's back early because "I got like three Incompletes? And they want me to finish them before classes start on Monday?"

Tricia was very impressed with Grant, I could tell. Wonders how someone "so on the fringe" could have hottie bf. I didn't *used* to be on the fringe. Or maybe there were just more of us on it back home and I didn't notice. Crowded Fringe.

Yes, another great band name.

Good night. I shouldn't be writing in here so much with Grant here, anyway, but he has been reading a text-book since 10, so who cares?

Went to Badicals meeting (mock run-through for tomorrow). It was sort of a shock to see WW III there. He was wearing this blue-and-red Nordic-type sweater, and he looked really, really cute. Forgot how blond he is. But never mind. I said hi and was really friendly, but I couldn't talk to him. I left before there was a chance of any alone time.

Later on Grant and I dropped by BF so I could pick up my paycheck and new schedule. Jennifer is running the place herself while everyone is on vacation. Said I had to start on Saturday. Or Monday at the latest. Monday, then. I asked how the holiday specials had sold and she said maybe there were some things better left to the Bagle Finagle main office.

Mmm. It is so nice to have Grant here lying next to me. But very crowded. Stupid single bed. Grant keeps insisting on coming to the meeting tomorrow to support me. I keep worrying about what will happen if Wittenauer is there.

This entry might need a parental advisory. Or there should be official notes about this somewhere taken by a secretary: not me. I should not be responsible for the official version. Too involved. Too many things happening at once. Agh!

All-day trustee meeting started at 10 A.M. Students wishing to make statements or requests had to be there at 1 P.M. I could not eat, and I drank too much coffee. Said good-bye to Grant and Mary Jo, who promised to come over and meet at the lecture hall and be there for my presentation. So Annemarie and I found the Badicals and we huddled outside the lecture hall, awaiting our turn. Wittenauer was not there and I was relieved. What if I botched the presentation in front of him? That would be awful, I was thinking. He'd lose all faith in me. Should have been the least of my worries. *Least.*

Dean S. came out at 1:00 to gather waiting groups. We went in. Waited our turn. I nodded at the long table of trustees on the stage and started to make my speech about wanting the college to not use "CFC" in any official capacity. I had 5 minutes and I filled it with important data so they'd be impressed. I also presented mock-ups of our new T-shirt design.

A minute or so later, Thyme/Morgan came in with some CFC 4-ever group, *including* Tricia (Incompletes? Complete lie!). I didn't even know Thyme was back yet. Turns out she was hiding out like a wealthy mercenary in a hotel suite, gathering her troops. She stood up and started presenting her argument to keep all the CFC stuff. "The CFC name has existed for over a hundred years, and it'll go on another hundred years, long past the day we're students here," she said, completely toeing the trustee line.

Then fur began flying. Whatever that means. She started pulling all this very familiar-sounding academic crap out of nowhere, about how it made sense we were doing this because it was a "rite of passage" to be "part of a counterculture," and how we were having a "role conflict" and we needed to be "resocialized," but the *sweatshirts* definitely didn't need to be redesigned.

"Wait a second," I interrupted. "Don't listen to her! She got that from my sociology notes! This isn't even an original *thought*!" Not only that, she was completely talking down to us.

Stupid photographic memory. I knew I shouldn't have let her look at anything of mine, ever.

She and I got into this screaming match about stuff, and she said I didn't take this seriously and had no convictions. She said she'd known I was a fraud ever since September because one time she counted the number of Slim Jims in a mug on Mary Jo's desk and Mary Jo was away for the weekend and yet the number of Slim Jims went down. Very embarrassing. "I didn't eat any!" I said. "I opened the package to see what it was *made of*."

Meanwhile another group had come in. Started telling us to get our petty concerns off the stage and get ready for a revolution. At this point, the trustees were looking worried. Caught Mary Jo and Grant sitting in the middle row of seats, also looking concerned.

"I'm sorry, but there are more important issues than this college's abbreviation," a guy at the front of his pack said.

Recognized his voice as the guy who had sprayed me with red stuff. Wanted to run over and punch him in the nose, see how he liked being sprayed with red liquid—only this time, actual blood.

"What is more important than saving what little is left of the ozone layer?" I asked.

"So there's a hole, okay, the EPA is working on that," the guy said. "What about the problems of economic globalization?" He went on with very impressive list of world problems, like dairy cows being cloned, and genetically engineered foods, and chemical warfare, and human rights violations, and the fact the CFC shirts might come from a factory that used child labor and sweatshops—his group was checking into that.

I glanced nervously around at my group. Erik and Annemarie were kind of shifting around, looking uncomfortable. Spray Guy was very impressive and smart.

Trustees' necks turning back and forth as if watching a tennis match, as everyone in the 3 groups argued. One of the trustees started having a flashback to the sixties. "What will happen if this escalates? We can't have violence on campus. We can't have tear gas and firebombs and the National Guard!"

295

"Which is why you should let the name stay the same!" Thyme insisted. "It's so unimportant in the grand scheme of things."

"Exactly. Because wouldn't you rather save the wild Arctic refuges from being drilled by oil companies?" the guy said.

"Definitely. That's the largest breeding ground for pregnant polar bears!" I added, getting sort of excited. "I mean, um, before they get pregnant. Whatever." My group was suddenly frowning at me, as I had apparently jumped ship, and was sounding like an idiot as I did it.

"But, ah, to redirect this discussion . . . how does that affect *us* here at Cornwall Falls College?" Dean Sobransky asked.

"Everything affects us," the sprayer said. "We're the future, whether you like it or not. And we have a responsibility to the planet."

"That's what we're trying to say!" I insisted. "That's why we don't want to *cheer* for CFCs. That's why we don't want anyone thinking that CFC is a good thing that should be put on sweatshirts and bumper stickers!"

Suddenly the door opened and a giant stalk of corn came running down the steps. Wittenauer!

"What is Corny doing here?" I heard Dean S. mutter.

I started getting really nervous as Wittenauer walked up past me and onto the middle of the stage, right in front of the trustee table. "Hello, trustees," he said. Then Wittenauer took off his corncob helmet. "It's me, Dean Sobransky," he said. "I'm Corny, and I completely support the idea to get rid of any and all CFC merchandise."

"Wi—wi—Wittenauer." Dean S. got purplish. Started stammering about Wittenauer's "unmitigated gall." "You're breaking a one hundred thirty-seven-year-old tradition of Corny being a—a—secret. How could you do this?"

"Because it's time to stop hiding behind a cornstalk. It's time to stop keeping secrets," Wittenauer said. "I think Cornwall Falls has lots of great traditions—but this isn't one of them." He started to strip out of his costume.

Dean S. slammed down a pointer he'd been using to illustrate, well, some point or other. "What are you talking about?"

"It's an elitist tradition," Corny said as he peeled off a husk.

Suddenly I realized he wasn't wearing anything underneath.

"It means that only the same kinds of people get picked, year after year. I got picked by someone just like me, whose dad went here, who was like a third-generation Cornwaller Faller. We're all male. We're all white. It's not fair." Another husk came off. Soon he was standing there bare-chested. Then he reached for the "cornbelt" that circled his waist.

"Please, ah, Walter, be reasonable," Dean S. sputtered as some of the trustees studied their notes and some watched eagerly. "We can discuss this in private. Is this really necessary?"

"Who cares?" one of the older women said. "Keep

talking, Corny, whoever you are."

"Walter Wittenauer." He smiled at her as he reached for the waistband of his green stretch pants. "The third."

Oh my God! I was dying. Was he really going to—?

Then he pulled off the pants.

Giant sigh of relief AND disappointment from the crowd.

He wasn't totally naked. He was wearing a pair of green-and-yellow CFC boxers. And he had put a red line through each little CFC logo.

"We need to change the abbreviation. We need to change the ways things are done," Wittenauer said. He turned to the More Radical Than Badicals group. "And yeah, we need to be more serious after this and work on bigger problems."

"Isn't he cold? Because it's like freezing in here?" I heard Tricia ask Thyme.

Dean S. cleared his throat. "If everyone could just give us some time. We need to discuss this. It's a lot to take in all at once." He took off his blazer and handed it to Wittenauer. "Come back in half an hour and we'll have some decisions for you."

"Better make that tomorrow morning," one of the trustees said. "We have a lot to discuss."

We all went out into the hallway. Wittenauer was standing there in a leather-elbow-patches blazer and CFC boxers. I just looked at him and laughed and ran over to hug him. I couldn't help myself.

Then I remembered Grant was there. Oops. Because

he and Mary Jo came up to hug *me*.

"So, this is, um, Grant," I said. My boyfriend from home? Even though I forgot he was here? "And Grant, this is Wittenauer."

"Walter, actually." He reached out to shake Grant's hand.

Is this what life is like for the Tom? Constantly introducing people he's kissed? I couldn't stand how nerve-wracking it was. Worlds colliding. Courtney freaking.

"Hi," Grant said. "Nice, ah . . . "

"Full Monty?" Mary Jo suggested.

We all laughed. I was actually impressed with the way Wittenauer and Grant were getting along. I admired them for it.

"So, do you think we have a chance?" I asked Annemarie as the group gathered around me.

"We didn't. Not until Mr. Maize here showed up." Annemarie checked out Wittenauer's muscular legs. "So. Been skiing much?"

Everyone went out for coffee, but I went back to the dorm with Grant. I should be so upset he's leaving tomorrow. But I'm not. I mean I am, and then I'm not. And I can't sleep. Too worried about what will happen tomorrow, next semester, next year, etc.

Grant is gone. I am crying, but for the wrong reason. I did the unthinkable today. I am regretting it already.

Grant was supposed to be leaving tonight, but he ended up leaving this morning. We got into this conversation over breakfast before our 2nd trustee meeting and the next thing I knew, I was telling him that maybe we should break up, because long distance relationships really didn't work. I said I couldn't help feeling jealous of him, when he was with Mary Jo, and I didn't trust him and Melinda, or him and Beth, or—or anything. So I didn't want to pretend that everything was okay being apart, because it wasn't. "When I come home this summer, we can start seeing each other again. But in the meantime, I don't think we should promise to be exclusive, because—"

"*You*, jealous? What? It's not me that you need to worry about. *I'm* so jealous of all the guys around you, I can hardly even breathe sometimes," Grant said. "Who is it? Is it that mascot guy? Is it one of those guys you work with—what's his name—Mark? No—Ben. Wait. Hold on. It's not *Ed*, is it?"

"No! I mean, they're nice guys. Great guys. But no, that's not it," I said.

"Then who?"

"It's nobody, Grant. It's me," I said. "I just can't. I feel like I'm living my life in these two different places, and I've got to choose one and just *go* with it for a while."

Grant looked so upset. Suddenly I felt like throwing up. What was I doing? What was I saying? I was throwing away Grant? The superiorest guy I've ever met (except for small slip-up) (still a factor, still bothering me).

"You're going to think about this some more, right?" Grant asked. "I mean . . . God, Courtney. You're not *serious*."

"Grant, you know me. Once I decide something . . . well, it's pretty much set," I said.

"Like how you decided we'd make this long-distance thing work, no matter what?" Grant asked, sounding angry and sarcastic all of a sudden.

"The no-matter-what part sort of got to me," I said. "I didn't think no-matter-what would include what actually happened. But Grant, look. This summer, maybe we can work it all out, maybe—"

"You know what, Courtney? Forget this summer," Grant said. "I'll make my own plans."

Then he left. Left! Drove away. Left me standing there in a snowbank. Zero compassion.

I still love Grant. I love him to death. But I can't go through another semester like the last one. Especially not in this weather.

Spent the day on the phone with Alison, Bryan, Mom, Jane, even Beth. Even Dad. "You did *what*?" was the common response. Mary Jo thinks I'm insane. I begged her to not tell Ed I am single now.

Anyway, trying not to focus on the negative. Trying to enjoy the "New Year's Resolutions for Cornwall Falls College" that were published by trustees after meetings concluded yesterday.

> **RESOLUTION 16**: to phase out the use of the initials CFC and to spell out the college name on all official clothing, in all cheerleader chants, in all university publications, and whenever and wherever possible.

If I wasn't so depressed over kicking Grant to the snowbank-covered curb, I'd be happy.

Another Monday morning at Bagle Finagle. Another New Product Team. New Product: THE CHEESE SHOPPE. Located within the walls of BF. Cream cheese not enough. We're going to sell wedges of cheese. Cheese fries. Cheese curds (both deep-fried and fresh). Cream of Cheddar soup. I swear, I don't get it.

Who wants cheese fries with their bagel? Who would come to *us* for cheese when there are specialty shops on the same block?

But suddenly it was really funny, because we were all back there: Jennifer, me, Ben (best co-worker ever, just named Assistant Manager), and Marcus (missed him on vacation).

"Courtney? Can I rely on you to be the Product Lead?" Jennifer was asking.

"What? No," I said. "I'm going to be really busy this semester."

"Well, then . . . Marcus!" Jennifer said. "You can be Head of Cheese. Or . . . Head Cheese. Or Cheesehead! Ha ha ha."

Mark/Marcus shook his head. "You can make me Assistant Manager if you want. Of *Apron* Redesign." He pulled one of the new bright yellow ones over his head. It said "Cheese All That" in black letters. "Who comes *up* with this stuff?"

"You know, Jennifer . . . we're going to quit if you don't stop introducing new products to run local family-owned stores out of business," Ben said. "You took on Brat Wurstenburger, and Brat Wurstenburger won. They're *still* doing great. Take that as a lesson, okay?"

"And what does a cheese shop have to do with bagels?" I asked.

"It's market research," Jennifer said brightly. She was over her burnout, back on her warpath. "I thought you'd be glad, Courtney. I thought you'd embrace the lack of meat."

Marcus had picked up a plate of cheese fries Jennifer handed him and dug in. "Oh my God. These are really good."

I stared at the cheese fries, resisting them. But feeling very, very weak. I walked over to the Blue Cheese Bonanza and took a whiff, just to kill my appetite.

Later, we all stared glumly into the new refrigerator case.

"If she even suggests putting brats *and* cheese *and* cheese curds in a *bacle*? We're going to quit. Right?" I said to Ben and Marcus.

"Oh, definitely," Marcus said.

Ben nodded. "We are so out of here."

"Me, too." I started stacking the napkins with the BF logo facing out. Every once in a while, though, I stuck one in backwards or upside down. I'm such an instigator.

6 pages left in this journal. Should probably start a new one to indicate new semester. Really should. But don't want to waste paper. New group in Badicals is going to focus on enforcing campus recycling and on saving the giant oak trees that circle the oval near the admin building, and on saving all trees from being killed.

Hope they don't make me sleep in those trees or strip to draw attention to the cause. Very cold. 5 below. Even Wittenauer would not strip today.

I must set an example for new focus group by reusing all half-filled notebooks this semester. Also I really need to cut down on printing e-mails and sticking them on my bulletin board.

Phone just rang. It was Dean S. Calling about a new work-study job for me. "But—the Funders," I started to say.

"Oh, no, this is a much more interesting and exciting proposition," Dean S. said. Proposition? I was starting to get very worried. "Also, a lot more hours. You won't need to keep working at that bagel shop. Are you ready?"

"Um . . . I doubt it," I said. Leave BF? Leave Ben and Marcus?

"You're going to be assisting the deans' offices. You're going to assist *me*, Courtney," Dean S. said.

I was highly suspicious. "You're just doing this so you can keep an eye on me, aren't you?"

"Just the same way I like to keep an eye on all our Cornwaller Fallers," Dean S. said. "Report to me on Friday at 10 A.M. All right?"

Do I get a helmet with this job? I was wondering. Dean S. is very dangerous to be around, constantly flinging and throwing things around. Got kind of depressed about losing the funding gig. Called Wittenauer to tell him.

"That's okay," he said. "I got shucked." He's no longer the mascot. "It's *such* a stupid job. But I just . . . liked it," he said, sounding really down.

"So you'll get it back," I said. "We'll protest. Don't even worry about it."

"They said I defiled the image of Cornwall Falls College and they couldn't be sure I wouldn't do it again," Wittenauer said.

"Well, good for you," I told him.

We started laughing and then he asked if I wanted to go for a walk. Was feeling adventurous, so I said yes. We went to see the actual Cornwall Falls. We walked. It wasn't that far—2 miles, maybe. The falls were unfortunately frozen over, just like everything else here. At first I was laughing because it seemed pathetic. Then I sort of had to acknowledge how pretty it was, thick crystallized ice, frozen tundra and all.

"They're really beautiful," I said.

"Yeah. I know," Wittenauer agreed.

We stared at the Falls for a while.

"You know, polar bears trap warmth against the snow with their fur," I said as my teeth chattered, repeating some line I'd heard on a nature special I'd watched 50 times.

"Is that a fact?" Wittenauer said, teasing me. "Let's try it." So we both threw ourselves onto the snowy ground to try to trap warmth—kept missing it. Kept trying again. And laughing.

Then we started walking back to town. Worked up a humongous appetite on the way. Needed hot food, fast. Ice crystals formed on Wittenauer's stubble. Sexy in an "Everest" kind of way.

First restaurant we came to was Brat Wurstenburger. Didn't even discuss it, just barged in past steam-covered windows and grabbed the table closest to the kitchen. I got the onion soup. Delicious with cheese on top. Forgot to tell waitress no cheese. Didn't care. At some point I realized this outing was sort of datelike, but not really. And then I realized I had a lot more guy friends than ever before, like maybe this was a "mat-oor" thing one does when one goes away to college. More guy friends, more weird friends, more friends who drink way too much milk.

So maybe there sort of could be something between me and WW III? But I'm not going to push it right now. Just because basketball season is starting up does not mean I should be Rebound Girl and leap into my next relationship.

"Oh yeah," Annemarie said when we were discussing it tonight. "Consecutive monogamous relationships make *no* sense."

Well, um, okay. So what else is there?

It's official. Mary Jo and I *both* have decided not to date anyone seriously this semester. Got too ugly and mixed up last fall. We're going to be single. Focus on classes (she was already doing that—I wasn't). Friendships. Checking account balances. We'll join more groups. Try out for some rec clubs.

"But you know, when all is said and done, I still think you should get back together with Grant," Mary Jo said as she chewed on a stale Twizzler.

"I know you do," I said. "But it's not going to happen."

"Yeah. Well, there's always my brothers. If it doesn't work out with Ed . . . you know. There's five more to choose from."

Threw Twizzler at her head. "Thanks. I'm sure Soren and I would be really happy together."

"Who?"

"Wait. Is it Kierkegaard? Or Hegel?" I asked.

"Who?"

"Maybe it's Wittgenstein," I guessed.

"I thought his name was Wittenauer," she said.

"Not *him*!" I said. "Your . . . never mind."

Still too embarrassed to tell her what I was trying to get at: name of 6th brother, who does not speak. Must sneak into her desk tomorrow and find out once and for all. If I can find her desk drawer handle under all the knickknacks.

Last page of a journal always makes me turn back to see where this all began. Started this journal missing Grant intensely. Still miss him. We made a pledge to stay together, to make our LDR work. Didn't know what I was getting into. Honestly.

How many pledges have I made and not kept? It's got to be in the hundreds by now.

On reflection, thinking about what I said to Grant . . . that whole "maybe by the summer" concept . . . I sounded exactly like annoying ex Dave with my stupid time line. Also I broke it off just as he was about to leave town, which I swore never to do.

Resolution: never sound like Dave again. Bad idea. Watch for Dave-isms in speech and seek to eradicate them.

And that whole thing with Mary Jo a couple of weeks ago about not dating anyone this semester. I mean, that seems *very* silly in retrospect.

Oops. That was yesterday.

Well, anyway.

Here's what I'd say to Grant if he could read this. But of course I don't want him to read this. Except for the last page. Which I could possibly tear out and send to him if I'm feeling adventurous and if this comes out halfway decently.

Dear Grant,

I was thinking it over, and maybe I was too hasty the other day. Not hasty, exactly. How about wrong? I don't want to be separated from you. Ever. And I don't know about this whole "exclusive" concept, but I'm willing to try again. I think.

What would you think of both volunteering at the humane society this summer? We could work together, and that way we'd get to spend more time together, which is really important.

See, I always kind of pictured us running this animal hospital, only I'm a real wimp about blood and body parts and singed fur and euthanasia.

But I could file, right? I'm really good with the alphabet. Remember: D comes before V except after C.

Love,

C.V.D.S.

P.S. In the meantime, how does spring break look for you? I was thinking maybe Cancun. Please get back to me ASAP.